FALCON TO THE LURE

From the open freedom of the English countryside where she spent an enchanted girlhood under the care of the aristocratic couple that she believed to be her parents, to the ancient nunnery where she sought sanctuary from the unholy forces of lust and intrigue with which the world threatened her, to the scented corruption of the royal Court, Diana Maundy had to follow a dark and twisting path towards the truth that was her birthright and her destiny.

CATHERINE DARBY

FALCON TO
THE LURE

Complete and Unabridged

ULVERSCROFT
Leicester

First published in Great Britain in 1981
Robert Hale Limited
London

First Large Print Edition
published 1999
by arrangement with
Robert Hale Limited
London

British Library CIP Data

Darby, Catherine, *1935* –
  Falcon to the lure.—Large print ed.—
  Ulverscroft large print series: romance
  1. Love stories
  2. Large type books
  I. Title
  823.9′14 [F]

  ISBN 0–7089–4097–8

Published by
F. A. Thorpe (Publishing) Ltd.
Anstey, Leicestershire
Set by Words & Graphics Ltd.
Anstey, Leicestershire
Printed and bound in Great Britain by
T. J. International Ltd., Padstow, Cornwall

This book is printed on acid-free paper

Part One

1

1394

That night Diana dreamed the dream again and woke with tears pouring down her cheeks and wetting the covers. Dawn was thrusting pale fingers into the room and the edges of the furniture were becoming sharper. She lay rigidly in her narrow bed with the hangings of dark velvet her mother had made, and waited for the details of the nightmare to blur in her mind. It was always the same, never changing in its sequence of events and the creeping horror that came nearer and nearer until she awoke.

Always, as she sank into sleep, there came to her ears the rushing of a river and, over and above that, the noise of tramping feet and lights flaring up into the darkness. She was very small, so small that she had to tilt back her head to see people's faces, and she was very frightened, so frightened that her legs shook beneath her. There were two people with her, a man and a woman and she clung to them silently, listening to the river and the marching feet. And then, inside her head, began a terrified screaming and for an instant the whole scene was lit up. She saw the river with the bridge spanning it and the monastery (she knew it was a monastery) crowning the tor, and the ragged men with desperate eyes reaching to drag her from her protectors. That was always the point when she woke weeping with relief because the dream was ended.

Now, as the crowing of the cock sounded from the yard, Diana stretched into wakefulness. Her room was a narrow chamber at the front of the house with its own winding staircase that led down to the side door that gave onto the covered passage. Its windows, glassed as were the other windows with tiny, leaded panes, looked out over the yard, and beyond the wall to the deep lanes and high hedges and rolling acres of Devonshire red earth.

The Maundy farmhouse was built of stone with ceilings of dark oak and a roof that was thatched every three or four years. Its main door opened onto a wide lobby with the shippen on the left and the kitchen and dairy on the right. Kate Maundy had the rushes swept out every month and prided herself on gleaming pots and pans and dustless tapestries. The staircase in the kitchen led up to the main bedroom where Kate and William slept, with a room for the maidservants opening out of it. The menservants slept in a loft over the stable, but the entire household ate at the long table in the kitchen, meeting at seven o'clock and five o'clock for breakfast and supper, with nuncheon at twelve being carried out to the fields or to the apple barn. Kate believed firmly that any ailment or unhappiness was best cured with plenty of good food and the Maundys set a generous table.

Diana was fully awake now, the tears drying on her cheeks, her mind calm. Her mother had always told her that bad dreams were caused by too much cheese on an empty stomach, but the girl wondered why, for her, it should always be the same dream. She shook off the last thread of memory and, pushing back the covers, swung her legs to the floor, her toes curling against the cool wood. The mirror against the wall was a small one and only showed bits of her at a time but she knew very well, from comments she had heard and the looks in the eyes of the farm lads, that the whole was very pleasing. She was tall for a woman and slim despite her mother's unceasing efforts to fatten her up, and her unpocked skin, blue eyes, and thick yellow hair evoked admiration. She wriggled out of her shift, rubbed a perfumed cloth over her face and hands, and polished her teeth with a slice of apple, before donning the day petticoat and the plain gown of russet wool that she wore on all but special occasions. Knitted hose and leather shoes completed her outfit and she bent, squinting in the mirror, as she combed her tangled curls and tied them back with a narrow ribbon.

She was expected to keep her own room and the shippen below clean, and to help her mother with the cooking. Those tasks occupied every morning, and when she had eaten her nuncheon she walked over to Father Anthony for an hour's reading and writing. She had been going to him for lessons for as long as she could remember, and could both read prettily and write a fair hand. Her parents were pleased she was intelligent because Maundy Farm was entailed and would pass to a distant male cousin eventually, and though she would have a good dowry it was to her advantage to brush up her accomplishments.

As she plumped up the pillows and smoothed the quilt her thoughts reverted to a conversation she had had with her mother the previous evening. After supper, while the servants cleared and her father checked the stock, she and her mother generally retired to the shippen where by the light of the blazing fire and the tallow candles they sat talking and sewing.

'You will be seventeen in a month,' Kate had observed, looking over the tops of her spectacles. 'A grown woman almost.'

Diana, who considered herself to be fully grown already, said nothing.

'We have plans for you,' Kate said, her round face gentle. 'Your father and I have splendid plans, for we are determined you will not spend all your life buried here.'

'Am I to visit London?' Diana asked eagerly. Her greatest ambition was to visit the capital where there were high buildings and streets crowded with people and shops full of beautiful things to buy and a wide river up and down which went brightly painted boats.

Her parents had stayed in London many years before and she never tired of questioning them about it. Now she asked again, 'Will it be as it was when you were there?'

'I hope not, my love!' Kate exclaimed, looking alarmed. 'When we were there the disturbances in the city were very frightening. The peasants rose up against their masters and stormed London, and nobody was safe until their leader, Wat Tyler, was killed and the king rode into their midst, crying that he was their true leader and would redress their wrongs.'

'King Richard,' Diana breathed.

'Aye, but he was a youngling then,' Kate said. 'He was brave and beautiful, and the country adored him. It is different now since his queen died and he quarrelled with his cousin, Henry of Bolingbroke. There are those who say that he means to make himself king one day but cannot yet risk open conflict, for many of the Court are still loyal to the true Plantagenet.'

It was exciting to hear her mother talk about these great personages as if she knew them. Yet she had only glimpsed them briefly, riding in procession to a service at Westminster.

'Do we go to London then?' Diana persisted.

'Perhaps. There is much to discuss,' Kate said vaguely and bent her attention to the doublet she was mending.

That had been the previous evening, and Diana had hugged the few sentences to herself with pleasurable anticipation. It was not that she disliked her home, it was simply that she had never been anywhere save to Exeter on market day. Exeter was a fine, crowded place but the very name of London had a magic glow about it.

Her chamber neat, she went down the winding stair and let herself out into the passage. The privies were against the outside wall, an innovation that William Maundy had introduced because his wife had a sensitive nose. Diana hitched up her skirts and went in briskly, whistling under her breath, a habit that her parents deplored.

The labourers were just coming in for their breakfast when she entered the big, warm kitchen where benches and stools were set at each side of the long table. Her father, thickset and jovial, was already in his high-backed chair and tilted his bearded face for a kiss.

'Did you sleep well, daughter?' he enquired. 'I dreamed,' she said truthfully, and saw his thick brows drawn down as he glanced towards his wife.

'Eat your breakfast,' Kate said, her voice high and bright. 'One is always the better for a good meal in the stomach.'

Raised meat pies, rashers of bacon, hot wheaten loaves, a crock of new butter, a jar of apple preserve, a dish of hazelnuts, two sorts of cheese, a bowl of buttermilk and a tankard of ale were arranged on the table between the wooden plates and the spoons. Diana, like her parents, had an earthenware plate and a silver tankard. She took her place on her stool and drew out the little horn-handled knife with which she cut her meat. A pleasant buzz of conversation whipped about the room, punctuated by laughter as the men quipped and joked. The Maundy household was a happy one, for William Maundy was a kindly man who took care of those who worked for him.

For the rest of the morning she was occupied with household tasks. Her mother insisted that no good ever came from idling and Diana was kept hurrying between kitchen, dairy and shippen. The summer fruits were at the peak of their perfection and had to be preserved and sugared for the winter. The linen had received its annual washing, but the tapestries needed to be checked for moth and the fish pond restocked, and apples had to be stacked and graded ready for the press.

At noon she ate bread and cheese and then taking her cloak from its hook, set off for Father Anthony's cottage. The old man was too feeble to walk far these days, but his mind was as acute as a man's half his age. He still offered Mass and heard confession, a rug over his knees, once a week, but for the rest he sat by the fire and read the half dozen books he had collected during his long lifetime, Father Anthony had a great love of words, rolling them in his mouth as if they were sugarplums. Despite his infirmities his sight and hearing were excellent, and he had a keen sense of humour sharpened by long observation of the people about him.

He greeted Diana with the gentle courtesy that was a feature of his nature and handed her the book that he had been perusing.

' 'Tis Master Chaucer's new poem,' he said. 'I have been fortunate to obtain a copy. Read it slowly now, for the words have a rare and rich flavour.'

She read, phrasing the words carefully as she had been taught. Most people spoke English these days though French was still the language of polite society.

'When April with his sweet showers
The drought of March hath pierced to
    the root
And bathed every vein in such liquid
Of which virtue engendered is the
    flower!'

Father Anthony, chin on his hand, listened with pleasure on his face. He liked young things about him and this maid was like the flower sprung from the dew of which the poet wrote. She would be seventeen in a month, he remembered, and hoped that her parents would not marry her off too swiftly before she'd had the time to enjoy being a woman.

'They are all going on a pilgrimage, are they not?' she interrupted herself to say.

'To Canterbury,' he nodded. 'There are to be stories from each member of the party but the work is not finished yet. Tom Darcy sent me this part from Exeter. I fear Master Chaucer makes sport of the Church but 'tis all in good humour. A little humour spices life.'

'I believe that I will be taking a journey soon,' Diana confided. 'My lady mother has hinted that we may go to London for a visit. Have you ever been to London, Father?'

'Once or twice, before I was ordained. I was a young man then, and the city is for the young. Bustling, hustling, always running and never getting anywhere.'

'But you've been here a long time, haven't you?'

'More than thirty years. I'm Devon born and so was granted permission to spend my remaining years in my native land. I was so frail in health that they didn't expect me to last more than a few months, but not even death is certain in this life.' His old eyes twinkled at her, and then he asked, 'Will you like going to London, do you think?'

'It will be an adventure,' she said gravely. 'I shall store up all the memories for my old age.'

'Hark at the young philosopher!' he mocked. 'You should enjoy life, my child, and leave memories to form as they choose.'

'Can a memory become a dream?' she asked.

'Yes, it can. Why?'

'I have a dream,' she said slowly. 'I have had it all my life, I think. I am with two people, by a river, with lights and marching feet coming nearer and nearer, but I am too frightened to run or to speak. And then there are men all about me, ragged men, with wild eyes and reaching hands. I wake then, weeping.' Unwittingly her hands had begun to shake.

'Dreams are strange things,' Father Anthony said. 'In them we meet our deepest desires and our worst fears. When the conscious mind sleeps then the soul stirs and weaves its fantasies. When we are young such rides upon the nightmare come often, but as we grow older our lives become fuller and we can deal more easily with our problems.'

He had not answered her question, she noticed. It had been the same when she had tried to tell her mother about it. Kate Maundy had given her an uneasy smile and told her brightly that a nice piece of apple pie would clear away the dismals.

'Have you any problems?' she enquired.

'If a man reaches the age of eighty-six without problems then he is either a fool or a liar,' Father Anthony said. 'It is the task of a priest to realise that his own personal problems weigh very light in the scales of human misery.'

'What was the worst thing that ever happened to you?' she wanted to know.

'Not something that happened to me,' he said, 'but to another. I saw a man burned as a devil worshipper once. Strangled and then burned.'

'Where was that?'

'At Canterbury, more than thirty years ago. I had been in poor health and my Bishop invited me to Canterbury with a view to discussing the details of my retirement. They were executing the devil worshipper in the cathedral square. He was a church man, an Abbot, which made it even more shocking. The crowds were very thick. It was hard to get through them, and I felt faint and sick, having taken a long journey when my health was low.'

'Did you see him, the devil worshipper?'

'He passed close to me,' Father Anthony said. 'An old man, very tall and aristocratic in appearance. There was great dignity in the way he carried himself. I was impressed by it, I admit. He seemed very calm, very scornful, as if he had chosen his path and did not regret it. Yet he was bound for hell fire. As an Abbot he must have known that, but he was unconcerned. And something in me said quite clearly that he was a better man than those who had condemned him. It was that conviction that made it so horrible, far more horrible than any dream.'

They were silent a space, then Father Anthony roused himself from his thoughts and tapped the edge of the thin manuscript.

'We must continue our work,' he said briskly. 'Go to the beginning of the poem again and translate it into French. Take your time. Languages are not to be leapt at as if one were a horse at a gate.'

Obediently she concentrated on the task, a little irritated because the old seemed to have a habit of breaking off in the middle of the most interesting conversation.

The lesson finished, she thanked the old man and went through the little graveyard with its attendant yews to the church. It was a small building that had stood since Norman times, its squat tower ornamented by a later hand with gargoyles, its oaken door scratched and pitted by generations of practising archers. It was her habit to come here, not because she was particularly devout, but because the church itself pleased her. She loved the glittering of the candlesticks on the altar and the red sanctuary lamp and the owls carved on the ends of the pews. Only the landowners sat in the pews. The labourers occupied the stools or sat on piles of rushes, their eyes fixed on the altar and the vivid statues of Our Lady and St Joseph. There was a narrow gallery at the back of the church where Jem Fiddler played for the choir to sing, and three windows of coloured glass showing the Trinity, with God the Father as an old man with a square red face, God the Son as a thin yellow figure on the cross, and God the Holy Ghost as a bright orange flame with stars all around.

Diana genuflected and crossed herself, then went slowly up to the altar rail and stood looking up at the carved wooden crucifix.

'One day when I am very rich,' she said aloud, 'I will buy a fine gold crucifix to match the candlesticks and bring it to Father Anthony.'

'You'll be more likely to spend on gold for yourself,' said a voice.

It came from the gallery behind her and for a moment she thought that God had spoken, and was so terrified that her throat closed up and her knees shook beneath her. Then she swung round and saw a young man standing looking down at her. The sun shining through the glass flung lozenges of colour over him, and she blinked, trying to see his face clearly.

'You're a pretty maiden to be talking to yourself!' the young man said, moving aside and beginning to descend the narrow stone steps.

'I was talking to God,' she said with great dignity.

'And found you were talking to me instead! Or do you think I am some citizen of heaven?'

He had moved out of the light and she had a clearer view of him. He was tall and paler than the labouring lads to whom she was accustomed, and his light hair fell straight to his shoulders under a cocked hat of green velvet. His short cloak of green swung from the shoulders of a tawny doublet and his long boots were, like his gloves, of doeskin. Diana supposed that he must be very rich, and then she blushed because his narrow green eyes, slanting above high cheekbones, were raking her from head to foot in a manner that her mother had warned her against encouraging.

'I don't think of you at all,' she said breathlessly, 'for you are a stranger to me, sir.'

'Then let me mend the matter. I am Maudelyn Falcon,' he bowed.

'God give you greeting,' she said politely.

'And you, Mistress — ?' He raised a questioning brow.

'Maundy. Diana Maundy.'

'A lovely name to suit a lovely face,' he said gallantly. 'You're from these parts?'

'My parents have a farm here, but we may visit London soon,' she boasted a little.

'Then, if you come to Court, ask for me,' he said promptly.

'Are you from the Court, sir?' But looking at his clothes she guessed that he must be.

'My father is Duke of Lancaster,' he told her.

'John of Gaunt? The king's uncle?' she breathed.

'The same. I am his bastard.' He spoke as if bastardy were something of which to be proud. Locally a girl in the family way was married off hastily, often after a good beating to teach her the importance of sin. Apparently rich folk regarded the matter somewhat more tolerantly.

'Does that make you a lord?' she asked uncertainly.

18

'Nothing so grand,' he said airily. 'I am plain Sir Maudelyn, having gained my spurs through my own efforts. My father taught me a long time ago that what we become depends on ourselves, not on our parentage.'

The idea pleased her, because it confirmed what she had always believed to be true.

'I'm bound for Exeter,' he said, 'but I stopped off to see the priest. There's no monastery here and I'm lacking a meal.'

She would have liked to invite him to the farm, but a shyness overcame her, and she said hurriedly, 'Father Anthony is in his house. He's very old but he loves company and he'll be glad to show you hospitality. Do you travel alone?'

'On private business for my father,' he said. 'I left my horse in the spinney. Did you know that you are one of the loveliest maids I've ever seen, in or out of Court?'

'Thank you, sir.' She dipped a curtsey, feeling the colour glow more redly in her face.

'And not betrothed?' He reached out and took her hand, turning it over.

'My parents have not arranged a marriage for me yet,' she said.

'So that is why you are being taken to London! Your father must have ambitions for you.'

'I think so,' she said, pulling her hand free.

'And I'll wager they don't include dalliance in a church with a bastard of Gaunt's,' he said lightly. 'I'll be off to your priest now, to see if he is ready for company and a bite of supper. You won't forget to ask for me if you come to Court?'

'I'll not forget,' she said, and watched him, wishing she had some excuse to call him back, as he bowed and went, graceful as a cat, through the door into the sunshine.

The beauty of the altar no longer held her attention. In her mind's eye was a richly dressed young man with eyes green as grass and hair that was the colour of wheat after the sun had dried it. He had said he was a son of Gaunt, and that made him a half-brother to Henry of Bolingbroke who, so rumour claimed, wanted to steal away the throne from King Richard. She wondered if the private business he was engaged on for his father had anything to do with that. Then she shrugged the thought away because it was not likely that any of it would ever concern her.

She bobbed to the altar and went out into the churchyard. Usually she lingered for a while in this quiet place, aware that it satisfied the deepest part of her nature, but she feared that the young man might notice her and believe she was waiting to see him again, so she went swiftly through the lych gate into the meadow that stretched its flower-starred acres to the lane that led up to the farm.

'You look worn out, child,' Kate said mildly as Diana came into the shippen. 'Do you have to run about all over the place as if you were a lad instead of a young lady?'

'There was a young man in the church,' Diana said, plonking herself on a stool. 'A very beautiful young man, from the Court!'

'Did he say so?' her mother asked.

'He is the son of the Duke of Lancaster,' Diana said. 'A bastard son, he told me, and he is bound for Exeter on private business for his father.'

'Then what was he doing in the church?' Kate demanded.

'He was going to visit the priest for a meal.'

'You should have invited him here. We set a more satisfying table than Father Anthony,' Kate began, then shook her head. 'No, the poor old man loves a bit of company, so you were right. Did the young man tell you his name?'

'Maudelyn — '

'Then it's not one of his bastards by

21

Catherine Swynford. Their names are John and Henry. His legitimate son is a Henry too, but I believe they call the younger one Harry. And Henry the elder has a lad called Hal. You think they'd find some new names, wouldn't you, but perhaps Court folk have more important matters to be worrying about.'

'He said that if I visited London I was to ask for him,' Diana interrupted.

'To London? And who said we were going there, Miss?'

'You hinted.'

'Aye, well, a hint's one thing, and doing is another! Not that we might not take a trip to London in the spring, mind! But you'll need new gowns. We cannot have you rustic among so many fine ladies.'

'And are we to go to Court?'

'We might, but there's nothing settled,' Kate warned. 'Your father would have to get a man in to oversee the spring planting, and there are the two apprentices due then. It never does for the master to be away when there are two lads to be trained up. But we'll try to arrange something, my lovely.'

'I would like to go,' Diana said and her blue eyes were wistful.

'In the spring then,' Kate said. 'Now go up and clean the ink off your hands and come down to the pantry. There's butter to be churned before suppertime.'

'Father Anthony had a new poem about people going to Canterbury,' the girl remembered. 'Master Chaucer wrote it.'

'New poems won't get the butter churned,' her mother said. 'Go and wash your hands and be quick, there's a good girl.'

Diana gave her mother a hug and ran up to her room. There was water and a cake of tallow soap on the table and she scrubbed her hands hard, watching the black smudges tinge the cloth. Kate Maundy was very particular about cleanliness. The whole family was expected to take a bath at least twice in the summer, and once every two months Diana had her hair washed in a mixture of rosemary and rainwater.

Her hands dried, she went over to the cupboard where she kept her clean shifts and the linen coifs she wore to go to Mass. Beneath them was her own private talisman. She had no idea where she had found it, or if anybody had given it to her. It had always been in her possession and, though months often went by without her looking at it, the knowledge that it was there gave her a warm feeling. Now she drew out the seal with its silver bird's claw the talons curled like the talons of a bird of prey. A falcon or a hawk? The young man's name had been Falcon. Maudelyn Falcon.

She whispered the name softly as if it too were a talisman, and the young man's face was as clear before her as if he were standing in the room.

2

It was decided that they would travel to London in the spring. Tom Darcy, an Exeter merchant with whom William Maundy did business, owned a small house there which he was willing to rent out for two or three months.

'And he will send me his own steward to oversee the work here,' William said. 'It's a great weight off my mind, for a man cannot enjoy himself with an easy mind if he has matters occupying him at home.'

The Darcys were prosperous folk whose two sons were already married, a fact that Kate regretted.

'For one of them would have served very well for you, my love. Fine young gentlemen, both of them. There is nobody to compare with them in the neighbourhood and Alice Darcy is one of my closest friends.

'She was in London this summer and has brought back accounts of the new fashions. Some of them are very charming, though I cannot imagine how one can get any work done with sleeves trailing along the ground! However, your father and I are determined to have you looking pretty.'

To that end they travelled to Exeter where William left them in the Darcy household for a week, and the two matrons sallied out to the town every day armed with lists of requirements for the long winter months ahead would be occupied in cutting and sewing the new dresses.

'Queen Anne has brought many comely fashions with her from Bohemia,' Alice Darcy chatted. 'Such a sad waste for her to die of the plague! The king is still not to be consoled, they say. You know he set fire to the palace of Shene, declaring none should ever set foot again in the place where he and his wife had been so happy?'

'A very foolish gesture!' Kate, who was a little less romantic than her friend, pursed her lips.

'And now he declares that he will not marry a grown woman but will take little Isabella of France who is only eight.'

'He would be wiser to beget an heir as swiftly as possible,' Kate said. 'His cousin of Lancaster has four sons and two daughters.'

'And like the king has just lost his wife,' Alice said. 'Is it not strange that both men should be born in the same year, both make love matches, and both be widowed at the same time?'

'And both covet the crown,' Kate added. 'Which is Richard's by right of birth, but Prince Henry will seek it by conquest if the king does not have a care.

'Now this is a sweet shade. It makes Diana's eyes and hair glow. You will have much ado to keep all the suitors away from her when you are in London.'

She was to have three new gowns, one of the bright blue that Alice Darcy was admiring, another of green and silver, and a third of dark red velvet. All the gowns were to have little pointed collars, hanging sleeves, and flowing skirts, and she was to have a coif of silver net sewn with pearls, and a coif of gold embroidered with jet. Diana would have liked one of the new butterfly headdresses with their trailing veils of gauze, but Kate declared they were for married ladies. She was, however, to have two cloaks of purple and yellow, and shoes of leather with modest points, and gloves lined with silk, and shifts, drawers, caps and petticoats, even a pair of leather corsets which pulled her waist into an astonishing thinness and were exceedingly uncomfortable to wear.

Winter was always a quiet time, with food carefully rationed and logs split for kindling and stacked under cover. The fields were bare stubble and the animals were penned in the barns and byres. Diana, who loved the sun, hated the driving rain that lashed the windows and the snow that looked so pretty on the hills but quickly became cold, wet slush in the lanes and yards. She still went two or three times a week to read with Father Anthony, but they spent much of the time talking.

'If you are to go into polite society,' the old man said, 'you must learn to conduct yourself as a lady should. You must take short steps and cast down your eyes modestly. When I was a young man a lowered eye and a closed mouth were considered to be marks of gentility.'

Diana tried her best, mincing up and down the priest's living room, her eyes half-closed and her lips tucked in, but despite her efforts to be solemn she could not refrain from giggling, and her jerky little steps made her look, declared Father Anthony, like a hen on springs.

'At least nobody will be able to find fault with your learning,' he said. 'Your reading and writing is in advance of most women and you pronounce the French tongue most charmingly. Your lady mother tells me you are most diligent in your household duties too, sewing a fine seam and producing a syllabub better than her own.'

'I don't suppose that Court ladies have to sew and cook,' Diana said.

'So Mistress Maundy plans to go to Court?' His eyes twinkled. 'How will you manage that?'

'There was a young man called upon you a few months since.'

'One of the Duke of Lancaster's byblows,' he nodded.

'I met him in the church,' Diana confided. 'He said that if ever I went to London I was to ask for him at Court.'

'I trust you will do nothing so scandalous,' he chided.

'The young man was very polite.'

'And, like many of doubtful lineage, amiss in his manner to a lady. I trust you snubbed him?'

'He seemed a most kindly young man,' she evaded.

'And handsome too.' He gave her a long look, noting her risen colour, recalling certain buried fantasies in his own youth.

'I will probably never see him again,' she said sadly.

'Better that you put him out of your mind,' he said kindly. 'These courtiers are free with their compliments, but it means nothing to them. And the young man will doubtless have business of his own to occupy his mind.

You know that the Duke of Lancaster is to wed Catherine Swynford?'

'No. No, I didn't.'

'His Spanish wife died and he is to make an honest woman of his mistress at last and force Parliament to legitimise their children. It will cause a great scandal but one has to admire the man for his faithfulness.'

'Maudelyn Falcon is not one of the Beauforts, is he?'

'No, he is the result of some casual affair. Gaunt acknowledged him but will not legitimise him. I fear that in Court circles morals are very low. There are those who declare the new fashions are to blame, with females painting their faces and lowering their necklines to encourage the men, but in my experience men have never needed much encouragement.'

'The world,' Diana said slowly and solemnly, 'is full of evil.'

'Full of sinning, child. There's a difference.' Father Anthony yawned, for he was tired and the reek of the fire weighed down his eyes. 'You'd best be off home now, for it draws into an early darkness with Yuletide nearly upon us.'

'And then will come the spring in London!' She laughed at the pleasures of her anticipation.

'You'll be a good, and obedient girl?' There was an undercurrent of anxiety in the sleepy old voice. 'Your parents have such great love for you, such hopes for your future. Everything they plan is for your benefit.'

'Yes, of course.' She gave him a faintly puzzled look before kneeling for his blessing.

Ever since the trip to the capital had been spoken about she had been aware of glances between her parents, of conversations that trailed away when she entered the room. At such times she was aware of the gap that yawned between childhood and adulthood, and longed to bridge it.

The landscape was desolate at this end of the year, the grasses frost rimed, the earth bare save for the clumps of flowering holly and the occasional splash of rowan. Here and there rushlight gleamed from the unshuttered window of a cottage.

Diana put her cloak over her head and set off across the meadow. The grey sky and the scudding clouds threatened rain and as she hastened her steps an owl swooped low overhead, bound on an early hunting expedition.

Fires blazed in kitchen and shippen when she entered the lobby, and there was the scent of meat roasting on the spit. Supper was nearly ready and the two maids were bustling about laying dishes and measuring out the salt. The men were in the dairy, shedding their boots and the thick, leather smocks that kept the east wind at bay.

In the shippen her parents sat at their ease, her mother sewing, her father with a mug of ale on the table at his elbow. They were talking in the easy, companionable manner of a couple long married and on terms of affection.

'No possibility of its coming out. 'Tis thirteen years since we were in London.'

William spoke soothingly, his free hand reaching to pat his wife's arm.

'You really think it won't be remembered?'

'In so much confusion? It is certainly most unlikely that anybody will recall us after such a long — oh, Diana, love, come into the warmth. Your nose is bright pink!'

His own face had flushed a dull red, though whether from the heat of the fire or because of the scrap of conversation she had just heard was uncertain.

'I think that this cloak would look good with narrow bands of sable to clasp it at the neck,' Kate said, rising to hold the heavy purple against Diana's shoulder.

'She will be the prettiest maid in London,' William said heartily.

'And if we are fortunate it will be possible to attend Court, to see the king and the great nobles at their supper or even dancing in the great hall at Westminster,' Kate said. 'If one of the duchesses were to notice you, why there might be a period of service in some grand household. That would be of immeasurable value to your future, Diana.'

They were talking brightly, their arms linked in hers as they moved towards the kitchen. She wondered what they had been talking about when she had interrupted them, and why her mother feared lest something be remembered.

The weeks of Advent passed slowly. Diana had always looked forward to Yuletide when there was a bright oasis of feasting and good cheer that lasted through the New Year until the cold fast of Lent plunged everybody into silence and darkness again. It was one time of the year when farmers and merchants, housewives and labourers came together in celebration. The church was decorated with holly and ivy, the purple cloths removed from the statues, and heaped below the pulpit were the Yuletide offerings for Father Anthony. Yuletide was a day for going to Mass in one's best gown, for walking or riding home across the stubbled fields to fresh baked bread, pies filled with minced liver and fashioned in the shape of mangers, goose basted with its own fat and swimming in savoury custard, goosegog tart and almond fancies with whirls of butter cream.

Later in the day they played hoodman blind and kiss-in-the-ring and exchanged small gifts, the bigger ones being kept for New Year when the fun was more secular. Much as she enjoyed Yuletide, Diana secretly considered New Year to be more exciting. On the eve of the festival the household sat in the kitchen and waited for the singing that began faintly, swelling as it drew nearer and the doors were flung wide to welcome the wassailers with mulled ale and apples polished red as rubies.

There was an unbearable, spine tingling excitement in the waiting for that chorus of far off voices to begin, even a moment's fear when the singing rose to a crescendo and died and all about the yard, glimpsed through a crack in the shutters, were the dark, waiting figures.

Then came the blaze of light, the shouted greetings, the kissing and hand-shaking, and when the ale had been drunk and the apples munched they all trooped across the meadow to where the Need Fire had been kindled, and warmed their hands at the blaze, and danced and leapt to feel the blood coursing through their veins and to know themselves to be alive even in the middle of winter.

This New Year was slightly different from all the others Diana had known. It was different because she was preparing to go to London, and some instinct told her that, afterwards, nothing would ever be quite the same again. She was imperceptibly drawing away from the things of her childhood, seeing the farm and the church very slightly diminished, as if she had already moved to a little distance. The visit would make her into a real lady, her mother said, and Diana knew that they hoped secretly she would wed some noble lord. At seventeen girls were ripe for marriage and her dowry, as her father had told her over and over, would be a generous one.

This year, as she moved out of the glare of the Need Fire, she remembered that Father Anthony had told her about the devil worshipper he had seen burned at Canterbury. It must be a terrible death, though Father Anthony had said the man had been strangled first. But suppose some part of him had still been aware of boiling flames and blackening flesh?

'You do be shiverin', my lovely,' a voice said at her elbow.

She turned, pulling her cloak more tightly

about her, and looked into the pocked face of old Marjorie Lanyon. Dame Lanyon had been comely once, with a husband and two fine children, until smallpox had wiped out her family in a week and left her scarred with wits a-wandering. She was harmless enough, but Diana, having the aversion of the young for those things twisted or deformed in Nature, generally avoided her.

'I am well enough,' she said shortly.

'And more than that, my pretty! Fair of face, you be. Fair as a pearl, or a crown of mayblossom. And you're off to London, they say?'

'In the spring.'

'Ah, there's something to dream on! A fine husband, d'ye think? A lord now or a merchant prince with a chest full of silver bars? You'll be married off, I'll swear. And no tears on this visit, eh? No weeping and grieving and coming back to whisper of secrets?'

'What secrets?' Diana asked in bewilderment.

'Secrets not to be told.' Marjorie laid her finger along her nose and winked.

'Pooh! you don't know any secret worth telling!' Diana said scornfully.

'I do, too! I do!' Marjorie's hand caught at her cloak, holding it fast. 'Such a deal I could tell if I'd a mind, my pretty!'

'Dame Marjorie, you've been overlong at the ale.' William, approaching them spoke sharply.

Under his frowning stare the woman dropped her hand, and stood, muttering under her breath, a sly defiance on her face.

'You'd best be off home.' William gave her a sharp push. 'And keep your mischief making to yourself, or there'll be no gleanings from my wheat for you when harvest comes.'

'What was she talking about?' Diana asked, watching Dame Marjorie stumble away. 'What secret could she tell?'

'None, poor soul. Her brain has been addled since she lost her family,' William said.

'She said she could tell a deal.'

'And all of it nonsense!' he interrupted. 'Now are you going to spare your poor old father a dance? When we get to London I'll have no chance, for all the young men that will come a-crowding!'

He was whirling her into the circle of firelight again, lifting her high, nodding his head and tapping his feet in time to the music of the fiddle. Her hair streamed out bright as a comet, her breath came in great gusts, and her question remained unanswered.

The Need Fire had burned low and the stars were paling when they started back to the house. Kate was rounding up the maids as if they were unruly fillies, for she was only too well aware that the lenience of New Year could lead all too frequently to a hedge get at Michaelmas.

The men were pissing on the fire to extinguish the red, remaining embers, and from the wall the cock crowed imperiously as if to remind everybody to hurry to their beds so as to catch a few hours' sleep before they all went to the first Mass of this New Year.

Thirteen hundred and ninety-five, Diana reflected, and felt the centuries roll out behind her. Each year was like a stitch in a vast tapestry, and nobody could move sufficiently far away to see the whole design.

She went to the privy, then climbed the narrow staircase to her room. It was, she knew, most unusual for a young girl to have a bedroom all to herself, but her parents had never had any children except her and they had done everything possible to make her feel as if she were the most important thing in their lives.

Her new gowns, one of them already complete, hung against the wall under wraps of white linen. They were like the ghosts of banquets that she had not yet attended, and she shivered again, aware that the room was cold and that everybody was so late to retire, it was unlikely that anybody would have remembered to put a hot stone in her bed.

From the next room she heard her parents talking as they prepared for bed. The partition wall was of wood, not stone, and she had often fallen asleep to the murmuring of their voices. Tonight her father's voice was slightly raised.

'Fool of a woman! I've a mind to have her driven off.'

'She's astray in her wits!' That was Kate's pleading voice.

'She'll be astray out of the district if she wags her tongue loosely again,' William said. 'All these years and not a word.'

'Perhaps we should tell, let her know the truth,' Kate said.

'No need, no need.' His tone was impatient. 'What chance of a fine marriage would she have if the truth were to come out now? I tell you, Kate, my dear, we risk all by speaking out.'

The voices sank and she heard the double thump of her father's boots as he dropped them on the floor. She blew out her own candle and curled up under the bedcovers, but it was a long time before she slept.

Dame Marjorie had a hut about two miles from the church. She had lived there alone since the epidemic that had killed her family, scratching a living from the land, regarded with pity by some, shunned by others. Diana had planned to ride over and see her as soon as possible, but on the day after New Year the snow began to fall steadily, obliterating landmarks, freezing the milk in the churns, patterning the windows with a delicate tracery of ice.

There was no possibility of riding out anywhere or even of walking far, though the family did contrive to get to Mass. That was more for Father Anthony's sake than out of excessive piety for the old man was never happy unless his church was packed to the door. In this bitter weather he huddled even closer to his fire, tottering over to the church with the aid of a stout stick and a lad who stayed with him from winter to spring to do the tasks that were beyond the priest's strength.

Winter was a harsh and bitter season, even in a prosperous household. The threat of famine was never far from anyone's door, and travelling was so dangerous that few ventured beyond the confines of the yard.

It was Candlemas before the thaw came, and Shrove Tuesday before the flooded lanes were passable. Diana, making the excuse that she intended to visit Father Anthony, saddled her pony and rode out, glad of the opportunity to be free of the stifling kitchen where, after long confinement, the various members of the household had begun to snap at one another over irritating trifles.

Dame Marjorie was perched on a stool, vigorously mending a hole in her roof, when Diana drew rein outside the hut. She looked down in a startled fashion, then bunched her skirts and jumped to the ground, skidding slightly as she landed on the mud.

'Good-morrow, Dame Lanyon.' Diana raised her voice slightly, fixing a smile to her mouth. She was a little afraid of the woman and felt afraid of her own fear, because poor Dame Lanyon was not to be blamed for her hideous face.

'Good-morrow, my lovely.' The woman regained her balance and bobbed a curtsey. 'Come to say goodbye to me before you go to the great city to catch yourself a lord?'

'I came to ask you what you meant when you said you could tell a deal,' Diana said clearly.

'Tell? Oh, I could tell,' Dame Marjorie bridled. 'But I promised that I wouldn't. I promised most faithfully.'

'Whom did you promise?'

'Master Maundy has been very good to me, very generous,' Dame Marjorie said. 'Poor widows have a hard time of it, and I'm grateful. I'd not want to be driven off.'

'My father wouldn't do such a thing,' Diana began, but the other broke in with a cackle of laughter, rocking back and forth.

'Who can be sure? Who can be sure, my pretty, what your father would do? Weeping and wailing they were and who can blame them! Poor Alice! Poor little Alice!'

'Alice?'

'So many die before their due time,' Dame Marjorie said. Her laughter had dried up, and she twisted her hands in the coarse wool of her gown. 'My man died, and the children, and there was weeping, and promises not to be broken, and poor Alice, poor sweet Alice.'

'I want you to tell me the secret,' Diana began, but the woman had turned aside, flinging her apron over her head, and moaning loudly.

It was obviously futile to question her. Mention of weeping only reminded her of her own loss.

Muffled by the capacious apron Dame Marjorie's voice declared sobbingly, 'I gave my word I'd not tell, and Master Maundy paid my heriot for me. I'll be driven off if I speak.'

'I'm sorry. I didn't mean to upset you,' Diana said, but Dame Marjorie had ducked into the gloom of the hut.

The girl waited helplessly for a moment, then rode away again towards the church.

Father Anthony was by the fire, as usual, and woke out of a doze to see Diana standing before him.

'Move aside, child,' he complained mildly. 'You're blocking the light.'

'Sorry, Father.' She sat down meekly, fixing her large blue eyes on him.

'Have you come for your lesson?' he enquired, fiddling for his spectacles.

'I came to ask you.' She hesitated a moment, then rushed on. 'I want to know if there is some secret about the time before when my parents went to London.'

'Secret? Why, what secret could there be?' he countered.

'Dame Lanyon knows of a secret, and my father told her to be silent.'

'Then you do wrong in trying to question other people about it,' he said. 'Dame Lanyon gets muddled in her mind. She has been muddled for years, and we must treat her gently on that account.'

'She lost her children, didn't she?'

'Her husband too, poor woman. He was a good man, and they had bonny children.

Robert and Bess were not ten years old when they were taken.'

'Bess?' Her glance was sharp.

'The little maid. 'Twas her death that sent poor Mistress Lanyon's mind into a spin. So you must not take notice of her rambling.'

'No, Father.'

'And you'll not trouble your parents,' he said. 'They are doing everything to give you a splendid future, my child. There are few girls as fortunate as you are.'

'I know,' she said soberly.

'Then ride along now,' he said kindly, 'and give my regards and blessings to your parents. You will be in London soon. I suppose that your preparations are nearly complete.'

'Almost.' She knelt for his blessing, and heard him say over her bowed head.

'When you are older and wiser you will come to understand that it is not always a good thing to ask too many questions, that it is sometimes wiser to keep one's curiosity damped down lest the fire burns one's fingers.'

'I'll remember,' she said, making her mouth prim, her eyes downcast.

Outside she mounted her pony and rode slowly across the meadow. Robert and Bess were the children who had died of the

44

smallpox. Bess. Not Alice. Not Alice for whom there had been weeping and wailing, and a secret never to be told.

'But I'll find it out,' she said aloud, her mouth setting into the determined line that few who knew her had ever seen. 'I'll find out what is to be found, I promise.'

A promise, even to oneself, was not lightly to be broken.

3

With spring came the journey. Even with fine weather and no delays they could not expect to reach London in less than a week or ten days, and William spent hours checking and rechecking provisions.

'Though we will lodge on the road a night or two, but the hostelries charge so dear for the simplest fare. Prices have risen so steeply these past years that I cannot fathom how people can afford to go anywhere!' he exclaimed.

'At least you can have an easy mind about the farm, dear,' Kate said absently.

She was counting linen and not much interested in the financial arrangements. In her experience men never ceased to grumble about the cost of living, but nothing ever improved as a result of all the complaints.

'Aye, Tom Darcy's steward will keep good account, and his wife will have a sharp eye to the conduct of the maids,' William agreed.

They were taking Jane with them and William had hired a travelling escort of two reliable guides. A party of six, riding by day along well-frequented roads could hope to arrive safely at their destination, and William was confident that he could give a good account of himself if any roving outlaws chanced to attack them.

Diana had little interest in her parent's concern over money and safety. Her whole mind was bent upon the great city, which, she saw in imagination as shining and magnificent, a kind of earthly Paradise filled with beautiful people. And somewhere in that city would be the green-eyed lad who had told her he was a bastard of Gaunt's. It had been such a brief meeting, but she could still remember his face clearly and the pleasant manner in which he had spoken to her while his eyes promised more exciting delights. Innocent but not ignorant. Diana sometimes found herself hungry for those delights, and decided that Father Anthony must be right when he declared that even the most chaste women had lewd thoughts.

She had not forgotten the question that troubled her most. The secret to which Dame Marjorie had referred and which had so irritated her father was still to be discovered, but she set the problem aside, instinct telling her that the answer would be found in London if she was meant to find it out.

They set off at dawn, each mounted, with three packhorses to bear the luggage. Kate was in a frenzy of anxiety at the last moment, the cow having rampaged into the vegetable plot and the hens having decided to stop laying.

'As if they knew we were going and wished to express their disapproval!' she moaned.

'Then the sooner we leave the more quickly will they settle,' William said firmly. 'Do mount up, my love, or we will lose time.'

Diana, already mounted, clad in a plain, russet travelling cloak, stifled a giggle as she watched her mother being hoisted to the saddle. Kate had put on a trifle too much weight, probably as a result of sampling her own cooking with overmuch enthusiasm, and she clung to the pommel apprehensively.

When they reached the top of the lane the girl glanced back and saw the sun gilding the thatch of the farmhouse and one of the dogs barking furiously as it reared at the gate, and the unbidden conviction came to her that it would be years and not months before she saw her home again.

The London road, free from ice and flood, was a broad ribbon up and down which travellers moved like streams of ants, flowing up and down, most on horseback, some walking, an occasional rich and elderly lady in a litter. There were groups of pilgrims, many wearing the cockleshells that proclaimed them to have made the long journey to the shrine of St James in Compostella. There were friars, riding plump donkeys and ready at the toss of a coin to preach a sermon or tell a bawdy jest. There were monks too, though Diana would not have taken them for such, many of them being in lay dress with armed servants and packs of dogs. A wedding party, the bride all in yellow, sped past, the horses decked with ribbons and bells. A troop of archers, faces and jerkins grimed, plodded behind a captain with a scowling face.

There was something interesting at every bend in the road, Diana thought, and the discomfort of hours spent in the saddle paled beside the joy of glimpsing other people, travellers like herself, bound for London or even further afield. Her parents were less enthusiastic. Kate loved her home and was never at ease when she was out of it, and the jolting of the saddle beneath her soured her usually tranquil temper. William Maundy was a man who enjoyed his food hot and well cooked, and the suppers at the hostelries where they stayed were often indifferently prepared. But there was something else that weighed upon them as they neared the city. Diana sensed it without knowing why, for both went to great pains to be cheerful, teasing her about the admiring glances of the two young monks who watched her as they passed, pointing out the various sights as they rode through the villages and little walled towns that signposted the way. But she could see the shadow at the back of Kate's eyes, and hear the faint uneasiness in William's voice when he laughed, and the realisation strengthened her resolve to find out what had caused it.

Apart from one brief shower of rain, that refreshed rather than soaked, the weather remained good throughout the journey. For Diana the indifferent food, the lumpy pallets, the uncertainty whenever armed men were glimpsed, were only part of the new experiences crowding into her life. Even her fatigue was pleasant for she slept it away each night and woke, full of energy, eager to mount up and ride on.

They approached London on the tenth day, having spent a night in a hostelry on the outskirts. Her first impression was of narrow, cobbled streets and high buildings, of a haze of smoke hanging over the steep roofs, of the sound of bells, and the smell of rotten fish, and the cries of hawkers, and the jangling of harness. Now and then the shout of 'Gardez l'eau!' heralded the emptying of a piss pot out of an upper window.

William pointed out the towering walls of

the Abbey and the new Savoy palace.

'Risen upon the ruins of the old which was fired by the peasants when they took arms against the masters. Your mother and I saw it burning,' he told her.

' 'Tis the Duke of Lancaster's property,' Kate said, and Diana looked at it with more interest, wondering if Maudelyn Falcon was somewhere within the walls.

They were approaching Temple Bar near where the Darcys had their London House. Alice Darcy had confided that it was in one of the better parts of the city near the great jousting grounds of Smithfield. Diana's first impression was one of faint disappointment for the house was a tall, narrow structure of wood with windows bulging under low eaves and no garden at the front at all.

'There is stabling for the horses at the end of the street,' William said, 'and a very pretty garden behind. Tom has had no difficulty in renting out the place when he is at Exeter.'

The small lobby opened into a long, low ceilinged apartment with a central hearth and a steep wooden staircase leading to the upper floors. The windows looked out over the walled garden at the bottom of which the river flowed past with its burden of small boats and flat bottomed barges.

Kate, seeming to throw off her despondency

was at once immersed in unpacking, checking that the bedcovers were not damp, counting the plate had been supplied and consulting with Jane as to what provisions must be fetched before a decent luncheon could be provided. William had paid off the escort and was on his way to arrange for stabling for the three months they had planned to stay.

Diana, finding herself with nothing to do, wandered down the garden to the gate that opened onto the river bank. It was clear that more people used the river than the road in order to move from one part of the city to the other. She perched on the low wall and watched with interest as the various craft went past, skilfully poled through the swirling current by men in dark blue smocks and cocked hats edged with gold.

'The Thames Watermen,' a voice informed her. 'They are very proud of their employment and brave too, for it takes courage to shoot the rapids at the bridge.'

'Courage for their passengers too.' She turned to smile at the young man who addressed her from the adjoining garden. He wore the gown of a student of law and his face was pleasant.

'There are very few accidents,' he assured her. 'I am Peter Todmore, and you must be one of the new tenants at the Darcy house.

We heard you were expected.'

'Diana Maundy.' She leaned to clasp hands. 'We are just arrived out of Devonshire.'

'So far a distance? Then you will be making a long stay. My mother has promised herself the pleasure of a courtesy call upon your mother.'

'We stay until the end of June,' she informed him.

'The city is unhealthy in the heat of summer,' he nodded. 'Those who can afford it move further out and pray that the plague does not follow.'

'There is sickness in the country too,' Diana said.

'But it does not leap from house to house so quickly. We are too crowded in London. But it's a fine city for all that. If your parents agree I would be happy to show you the sights. You will want to see the lions at the Tower, and a bear baiting, perhaps? Ladies often weep for the bears but 'tis fine sport. My own bretrothed declares that she prefers it to the cockpit any time.'

'Betrothed?' she enquired with lively curiosity.

'And due to be married as soon as I'm called to the Bar in a year or two. You'll like Enid. She's fifteen, five years younger than I, but comely and sensible.'

'Does she live in this part?'

He shook his head. 'Enid lives in Cheapside. Her father, Ralph Aston, is a wool merchant there. She's a twin brother, Giles, who'll inherit the business. He's apprentice now to his father.'

'Is he betrothed too?'

'Not yet. Master Ralph thinks him too young to be tied. In faith, you ask so many questions you should have been a lawyer!'

'I have an inquisitive mind,' she said, dimpling at him.

'And a lively wit! I like a girl with a lively wit.'

'Diana! Diana, where in the world have you — oh, there you are! Sitting on the stone which is likely damp from the river and ready to give you the ague before your time!' Kate, grumbling loudly, hurried down the garden.

'Mother, this is Peter Todmore who is to be called to the Bar as soon as he is due to wed,' Diana said, scrambling down.

'Todmore?' Kate came to a stop just within the gate. 'Do I know your family? Have you lived in these parts long?'

'Ten years, mistress. We came from Suffolk.'

'Oh, then you won't — ' She drew herself up with a breathless little laugh. 'I was going

54

to say that you wouldn't have been here when my husband and I visited London before. There were fields about the house then, but it's been built up since.'

'I think most of the neighbours have moved in since we came.'

'And your name is Peter Todmore? I hope I shall have the pleasure of meeting your parents.'

'My mother intends to call upon you,' he said. 'I have been telling Mistress Diana here that I would be happy to show her something of the city while you are here. My sweetheart and her brother live in Cheapside and we often make up a party with other younglings.'

'To see the lions in the Tower or a bear baiting,' Diana said eagerly. 'I may go, may I not?'

'If your father agrees. But you must come in now and help me. There were not sufficient provisions left for us in the house, and we'll have to bestir ouselves to market if your father is to have a worthy supper. What was that?'

She jumped as a dull boom echoed across the water.

'The royal salute,' Peter said. 'His Grace is coming from the Tower. He holds Court at Westminster this month.'

'Do let us wait to see him pass,' Diana begged.

'Very well.' Considering, Kate nodded. 'Your father saw him when he was a lad, riding alone to talk to the peasants. William always said it was a brave sight. And I myself had a glimpse of the king's mother. The Lady Joan of Kent she was. A very beautiful lady.'

'Is that the royal barge?' Diana was on tiptoe, shielding her eyes from the sun that dazzled upon the river.

'The sovereign escort. The royal barge flies the white hart banner, which is the king's personal emblem,' Peter informed her.

'There it is! I see it!' Diana shrilled, almost overbalancing as she craned her neck. 'I can see the white hart banner. And that must be the king! Oh, do look, mother! It is the king, isn't it?'

'With the Duke of Lancaster,' Peter said.

'John of Gaunt?' Diana narrowed her eyes at the tall, bareheaded figure who stood behind the gold upholstered chair on which a slim man robed in crimson sat, the sun striking fire from the golden circlet on his red hair.

'He wears armour whenever he comes into the city,' Peter said. 'The Londoners hate him, but he has only contempt for them.'

'The king looks contemptuous too,' Diana said, staring at the pale faced man who, head erect, looked neither to left nor right.

'They say the death of Queen Anne affected him greatly,' Peter said.

'Poor King Richard,' Kate said softly.

'At least he can rely on his uncle of Lancaster's fidelity,' Peter said. 'There is little love lost between him and his uncle of Gloucester, and less between his cousin Henry of Bolingbroke and his nephew Thomas Mowbray. The king lacks an heir and many cast envious eyes upon his throne.'

'Should a lawyer speak so free?' Diana asked.

'You are quite right,' he said, 'but I am not fully fledged yet, and so may be pardoned a small indiscretion? Mistress Maundy, I will go back and tell my mother that you are come. She will call upon you tomorrow.'

'The house will be straight by then, and we will be recovered from the journey,' Kate said. 'Come along. do, Diana! There is no time to be spent in gazing at the river.'

The royal barge had passed, the armour clad figure bending to speak to the crimson robed monarch who sat so still that he might have been a waxen effigy instead of a living being.

'The market is only a step away,' Kate declared, bustling her daughter back to the house. 'We shall require ginger and a couple of spring chickens and bread, and to tell you the truth I'll not trust that oven until I've cleaned it out with my own hands. Good day to you, Master Todmore. I shall look forward to meeting your parents.'

'And I can go to see the lions at the Tower?' Diana asked.

'If your father says that you may.'

'And to see the bear-baiting?'

'We'll see, we'll see. Come and sponge your hands and face and tidy your hair. You and Jane can step over to the market together and buy what we need. You are quite old enough to bargain for fair prices.'

Diana waved her hand to Peter Todmore and went indoors.

Half an hour later, money in her purse and Jane lugging a large basket, she set out. Kate had given her directions, and a short walk brought her to the open market place where booths and stalls and penned animals were jumbled together.

With Jane trailing behind, Diana went from stall to stall making her purchases. She suspected that people, hearing her country accent, overcharged her, and the two chickens she succeeded in buying were poor specimens compared with the ones they reared on the farm, but there were bewildering varieties of spice and pickle, and she was tempted to buy more than was written on the list.

It was when she reached for her purse in order to obtain a pretty stone jar filled with lumps of green ginger that her fingers clutched at the end of a dangling ribbon.

'Someone took my purse!' She exclaimed aloud in dismay. 'I never felt — Jane, did you see anyone?'

'No, nothing. Someone jostled me,' the maidservant said, her eyes wide.

'Market's full of thieves, mistress,' the stallholder said, sympathy in his voice. 'They work in pairs, one to distract the lady's maid, the other to cut loose the purse. And they're gone in a twinkle.'

'Did you have much money in your purse, mistress?' a bystander asked.

'Enough to buy the green ginger,' Diana said mournfully.

'Then you must allow me.' He tossed a coin to the stallholder and, lifting the stone jar, gave it to her.

'But I can't accept!' Her face flushed as she stared up at the man. He was in middle-life, thick fair hair streaked with grey, dressed with a sort of careless elegance that matched his swaggering gait.

'I am newly come from France, mistress,' he said. 'It does my heart good to give a present to a comely wench, and I'd not have you think that all Londoners are rogues.'

'It's very kind of you sir.' She dipped a grateful curtsey, and he smiled and swung through the crowd.

'That's a handsome knight!' Jane breathed.

'We'd best get back.' Diana added the jar of ginger to the other purchases in the basket, and said, somewhat crossly, 'Do close your mouth! We'll be robbed and cheated all over the place if we walk about with our mouths agape!'

'Yes, mistress.' Jane giggled and followed her.

It was sliding fast into afternoon and Kate would need the provisions but she lingered, pausing to admire a stall on which fine lace was displayed. The old woman who sat by the stall lifted up a piece and held it out for her inspection.

'Handmade, mistress, and the best quality,' she invited. 'It would make a lovely coif.'

'Yes, it would, but I've no money left,' Diana regretted.

'I'm here every day,' the woman said. 'You're a stranger, aren't you?'

'And have been robbed already,' Diana admitted. 'I shall have to use my brains or be taken for a gull whenever I step into the street. But I'll ask my lady mother if I can come back and have the lace.'

'From the West Country, aren't you?' The old woman was evidently eager to chat, perhaps because there were no other customers waiting.

'From Devonshire. We're staying here in the city.'

'I recognised the accent. There were some nice people from Devonshire who stayed here years ago. The lady bought some of my lace. Very sweet manners had Mistress Maundy for she would often stop to enquire how I did.'

'Mistress Kate Maundy! But that is my lady-mother's name!' Diana exclaimed.

'Never! Then you'll be little Alice!' The old woman clapped her hands together, her face beaming.

'Alice?' Diana's own smile faded.

'I can see you now,' the lacewoman said. 'Holding onto your mother's hand and begging for a bit of marchpane to suck. Three or four years old you were, and smart as a cricket! She brought you two or three times while she was staying here and always stopped to pass the time of day. I often wondered what happened after the troubles. The peasants stormed the city, you know, and there was much disorder. I suppose your parents went back to Devonshire, for I never saw you or Mistress Maundy again. And here you are grown into a fine young woman! Little Alice Maundy!'

'I'm late. I have to go now,' Diana said, bobbing her head and hurrying away. At her heels Jane said,

'Why did she call you Alice?'

'She's old and muddled,' Diana said hastily. 'You'd better not mention it to my mother. She'll be angry at our wasting time in gossip.'

Kate was, in fact, in a state of considerable agitation, having just discovered that she had neglected to pack her most comfortable pair of slippers. The corn on her little toe fitted very neatly into the worn slippers and were a blessed relief after a day on her feet.

'Though a day on one's feet is preferable to a day in the saddle,' she said. 'You got everything on the list?'

'We were robbed,' Jane said.

'What! In broad daylight? What happened?' Kate demanded. 'Diana, surely you're old enough to be trusted to go to market without beggaring me!'

'I'd bought everything except the ginger,' Diana said. 'A man pushed Jane and another must have cut my purse loose.'

'But you've got ginger.'

'A gentleman saw what happened and insisted on buying me some.'

'A knight just back from France,' Jane slipped in.

'You ought to know better than to go talking to strange soldiers,' Kate scolded. 'This is London, child, and country manners are not suitable here. Now go upstairs and change your dress. Jane, get those chickens plucked and drawn. They're so thin I'll swear they died of starvation. Oh, and Diana, I had a word with your father and he's just stepped over to make himself known to the Todmores, so it's likely you'll be allowed to go and see the lions in the Tower, but don't worry him with tales of being robbed and of knights from France buying you pots of ginger!'

'I'll not say a word,' Diana promised, kissing her mother and escaping thankfully upstairs.

The chamber where she was to sleep was smaller than her room at home and bare of tapestry, but its windows opened out over the long garden with the river beyond.

Diana took off her cloak and sat down on the narrow ledge. So many things had happened in the short time since their arrival in the city that she craved leisure to reflect on them. Peter Todmore had seemed to be a courteous young man, and she fancied she would enjoy going out with other younglings. On the farm she had not felt the lack of companions, but she sensed that in London it might be lonely without friends of her own age.

She had actually seen the king! That alone was something to remember if His Grace came so seldom to his capital. She supposed he had to show himself in other parts of his kingdom in order to defend it against those who would usurp it. The Duke of Lancaster's own son was one, and yet the duke stayed loyal to his nephew. There was honour in that, Diana considered, and wondered if Maudelyn Falcon had been among the little group of nobles clustered about the king.

Then there had been the man who had given her the ginger, and the lacewoman, who called her Alice and recalled her begging for marchpane.

Dame Marjorie had spoken of little Alice too, and of mourning and weeping, and Father Anthony had warned her not to ask questions.

'But I am Diana, not Alice,' the girl muttered. 'I am Diana, and nobody mourns for me.'

She looked about the room, trying to

stir some buried chord of memory. She must have been here before and that was another strange thing. Her parents, on the rare occasions when they mentioned their previous visit to London, had never spoken of her having been with them. She had always assumed that she had been left in Devonshire.

Into her mind, without warning, came the name Becky. Becky, screamed over and over as the men closed in. Becky? It was a name she had never even heard spoken, and now it was as clear in her mind as if someone stood at her elbow and tugged at her sleeve.

She rose abruptly and went over to the saddle bag which still stood unpacked against the wall. She pulled loose the straps and tipped stays and hose over the floor, groping for the seal. Not until her fingers closed over the silver of the falcon's claw did the name of Becky stop screaming inside her head.

4

A few days later, with her father's permission, Diana went with Peter Todmore to meet his sweetheart and her brother and to spend the day at the Tower. They were to go by boat to Tower Wharf where the others would be waiting and Diana took her place with a certain amount of apprehension. She had never been on a river in her life, and she was not at all sure that she would be able to get out of the boat without tumbling into the water.

'Enid and I are cousins of a sort,' Peter told her. 'My father is a cousin of Enid's mother, so that makes us relations. Her mother is older than her father, about ten years older. I wouldn't wish to take a wife older than I am.'

'Nor I a younger husband?' she agreed.

'You are not betrothed?' He looked faintly surprised.

'Nothing has been arranged yet,' she said.

'Perhaps they plan to wed you to some noble gentleman,' he joked.

'Perhaps.' She changed the subject, pointing ahead of them down river. 'Is that the bridge?'

'And the Tower is beyond. You will see it clearly in moonlight. What ails you?'

'Skulls,' she said, her voice shaking. 'Skulls fastened on the bridge!'

'Heads of felons and traitors,' Peter said, dismissing them. 'Hold on now. We are going to shoot the rapids.'

She shut her eyes and clung to the rope, hearing the boatman's triumphant shout as they plunged down into calmer water. Opening them, she saw the high walls of the great fortress looming behind, before them and on the wharf two figures waving.

'Take your time. The landing stage is slippery,' Peter warned.

She stood up cautiously, avoided looking down at the heaving water, and stepped up to the wharf.

'Enid, Giles, let me introduce Mistress Diana Maundy,' Peter was saying.

She shook hands politely with the two brown haired younglings.

Their resemblance was so marked that it was easy to see that they were twins, though Giles was slightly taller and heavier.

'My mother has invited you both back for a meal,' Enid said. 'Giles has been given the whole day free, so we have ample time in which to enjoy ourselves. Are we going to see the lions first?'

'I never saw a lion!' Diana looked eagerly up the slope to the massive gates.

'The Lion Tower is just within the entrance,' Peter said. 'They have leopards and bears too, and monkeys, and birds, and snakes and lizards.'

'And an elephant,' said Enid. 'It's dead now and stuffed, but you never saw anything so fearsome!'

The lions were as magnificent as Diana could have hoped. She gazed, fascinated, as they paced behind the bars of their cages, powerful muscles rippling under their tawny coats, tails swishing. She had never seen such splendid animals in her life and yet it seemed sad that they should be prisoned.

'Are you not afeared of them?' a tall man enquired. 'Not when they can't get at me,' she said.

'A wise maiden.' He stepped back a pace and looked at her more intently. 'Not a stranger either. We've met before.'

'In the market place. I owe you for a pot of ginger.'

'You may pay me another time, Mistress — ?'

'Maundy. Diana Maundy. I am staying with my parents at the Darcy house near Temple Bar.'

'Then we will have the pleasure of meeting again.' He swept off his feathered cap and bowed. 'Your friends are waiting now, and scowling as if I contemplated an abduction!'

He was gone before she could reply, and Peter, who had moved on to look at a leopard in the next cage, was tapping her on the arm.

'I thought you didn't know anyone in London,' he observed.

'I don't. That gentleman helped me in the market, and chanced to be here today. He is just come from France.'

'The city is full of rogues. Your father won't thank me for putting you in the way of one,' Peter said.

'He seemed very polite,' she said, returning his slight frown.

Law student or not, he was, she considered, in no sense responsible for her behaviour. She was determined to speak to whoever she pleased without asking his permission.

'Do come and see these bright birds,' Enid invited, hurrying back to them. 'They are the most fantastic colours you ever saw!'

'Enid never tires of the birds,' Peter said. His face relaxing, he put his arm about her and moved onward. As she followed them Diana looked about for the tall knight but there was no sign of him.

'There are gardens within full of rare plants,' Giles told her. 'I've a mind, when

69

my apprenticeship is done, to dye some of my cloth in the colours of the flowers. I would like to expand, to experiment a little with various methods of dyeing the wool so that the shades don't run when the garment is washed.'

His rather heavy face was alight with interest. Diana warmed to him a little more, for she had the wit to appreciate enthusiasm when she came upon it.

As they strolled with the crowds through the arched passageways with their borders of vivid flowers, she glanced up at the narrow barred windows at which an occasional face could be seen. On the leaded walks that ran between the towers armed guards slowly paced. It was a reminder that this was a State prison, and that dark deeds as well as flowers flourished in this place.

She averted her eyes and looked instead at the graceful palace that spread its walls below the square Keep of the White Tower. The doors to the Great Hall were open and guides were ushering the spectators through the public apartments. She had never seen such high ceilings, such an expanse of intricately worked tapestry, such gilded stools and tables, such finely wrought goblets and elaborate salt cellars.

'Visitors are not allowed into this part

when the king is in residence,' Enid said. 'But His Grace is not here very often. He stays mainly at Westminster.'

'If I had recourse to such a palace,' Giles said. 'I would take full advantage of it.'

Diana, glancing round, was less certain. She thought that even in this luxury she would not be able to forget the grim barred windows and the armed guards above the walls.

They came out into the gardens again, and bought some chestnuts from a stall, and went back to have another look at the stuffed elephant. Diana enjoyed herself, for the morning was fine and warm and the people about them were in holiday mood.

Afterwards they strolled along the river bank, watching the boats and barges and little fishing smacks. There seemed to be trading carried on everywhere with flocks of sheep being driven among the crowds, men with scythes and pitchforks offering themselves for hire, furred merchants on plump geldings, archers on leave from the wars with their painted doxies clinging to their arms, and everywhere the beggars crying for alms as they displayed their rotting sores.

'Painted on for the most part to excite pity,' Giles said stolidly, leading her around

71

a cart piled high with apples. 'We will walk back towards Cheapside, though there is nothing of much interest to be seen.'

To Diana everything was of interest, though she would have sacrificed the smells and the yellowish grey pall of dust that hung over the roofs.

'For everybody burns coal these days,' Peter informed her. 'Sea coal is brought from the north east and burns with a slower, hotter flame than wood or peat.'

'And stinks more!' Enid cried, holding her nose and grimacing. 'When Peter and I are married I shall moan for a house beyond the city walls with a garden running down to the river, and I shall spray perfumes in every room.'

'Then I shall have to accept bribes in order to afford my wife!' Peter exclaimed.

They had turned into a long, winding thoroughfare, with houses leaning together and many windows bulging out over the lower storeys. It was more crowded here than in the gardens of the Tower, and they were frequently jostled and pushed, or forced to sidestep a deep puddle or pile of refuse.

'This is my father's house,' Giles said, with a note in his voice that reminded them that one day it would belong to him.

It was a tall, narrow building, very similar

to the one where the Maundys were staying, but with a large window by the door in which rolls of woollen cloth were displayed. Enid pushed open the door into a narrow lobby and called down the passage.

'Father! Father, we're here!'

A man of middle height, his hair greying, a long gown making him look older than his years, came from what was evidently a storeroom at the back, and shook hands cordially.

'Mistress Diana, Peter told me that you were staying at Temple Bar near to his own house.'

'With my parents, yes.'

'Then it will be pleasant for you to see some of the sights of London with Enid, and Giles too when I can spare him. He has work to do if he is to complete his apprenticeship, but an occasional day's holiday never did anybody harm.'

He looked, thought Diana, as if he seldom took a holiday himself. There was a greyness about him as if he had spent too long among his own bales of cloth.

'Mother will be upstairs, laying the meal,' Enid said. 'Giles, do show Diana the garden, while I prepare her for our arrival. You know how Mother gets if anybody walks in on her unannounced.'

'We do have a very pretty garden here,' Ralph Aston said. 'My lady wife is a very clever gardener. Very clever indeed. Come and see it, Mistress Diana.'

She went politely through the dim, storeroom into a garden heavy with flowers and herbs, with a vine trained over the brick wall and gillyflowers clustered thickly along its top. At the bottom of the garden a pear tree spread crooked branches over a stone bench.

'It is very pretty' Diana said.

'But not to be compared to your beautiful Devonshire countryside, eh?' Ralph Aston said.

'There are more people here,' she admitted.

'And many of them rogues. My father was a Norfolk man but he settled here as wool merchant. He and my mother fled to Kent when the black death came and perished of it. I was only a babe.'

'Then who reared you, sir?'

'A woman called Dorothy. A good woman. who ran the business till I was of an age to be 'prenticed. She died some years since but we visit her grave at each anniversary. Now you must come upstairs and meet my lady wife.'

Mistress Aston was in the living quarters on the upper floor. A small, thin woman, in a gown that was a little too bright for her years, she shook hands briskly and proceeded to urge food upon them all as if they were celebrating the end of a siege.

Diana's head was beginning to ache by the time the meal was over, for as she ladled and carved so Mistress Aston talked, chatting on and on with scarcely a pause for breath.

'Not that I ever jaunt to the Tower myself, but Enid does enjoy an outing, and it is good for a maid to take the air upon occasion, though to hear some people talk you would think there was no air in London! I am firmly of the opinion that coal smoke is a preventative against the plague, and a little cinder water is an excellent remedy for the wind. You must pass my hint on to your lady mother, my dear, for if she is like me she will be glad of such a remedy, females at our time of life being subject to certain discomforts, not to be mentioned before gentlemen, but Peter will excuse me, for he is one of the family already, not only because he is to marry Enid, but because his father and I are cousins. Are you from a large family, my dear?'

'No. There are only my parents and me.'

'Then it must be a great treat for you to mingle,' Mistress Aston said with faintly irritating kindness.

'But we must not keep her too long from her parents,' Master Aston said. 'They may be anxious if she is late home.'

'I am not expected back so soon,' Diana began, but her hostess was on her feet at once, reaching for cloaks and hoods.

'Peter and Giles are engaged to watch a cockfight,' Enid said. 'Shall I walk back with Diana, or shall we take a boat?'

'I'll escort Mistress Diana,' her father decided. 'You will not object a small detour? It is the day when I lay flowers on Dorothy's grave.'

'But who is to watch the shop?' his wife questioned. 'If Giles is at the cockpit, and you are out, how shall we contrive?'

'Cannot you and Enid manage between you?' Master Aston enquired, a faint weariness in his tone.

'I suppose we could, if you are no longer than an hour or two,' she said doubtfully.

'I could find my own way,' Diana put in. 'At home I often went out alone.'

'But not in the city, my dear. It is no place for country maids,' Master Aston said.

'You will come again soon. Perhaps we could row to Chelsea,' Enid said. 'There is a very pretty village there where one can buy early strawberries and eat them with cream.'

Diana said truthfully that she would look forward to that, thanked Mistress Aston for the meal and the younglings for their company, and followed Ralph Aston out into the street.

Away from his wife's chatter he seemed to relax a little, pointing out various shops and houses to her as they went along, pausing occasionally to bow to an acquaintance.

'The nobility pride themselves on their wealth and power,' he observed, 'but I am certain that the future of England is in the hands of the merchant classes. It is upon us, and upon the yeomen farmers, that stability will depend. Mistress Dorothy often used to say that to me; I thought her words wise then, and think them wise now.'

'You were fond of her?'

'Very much attached,' he nodded. 'She was a childless widow who devoted herself to my interests. She was past seventy when she died, but she retained her faculties to the end.'

'I don't think I would like to live to be terribly old,' Diana frowned, 'even with all my faculties.'

'You will feel differently,' he promised, 'when you approach forty.'

'Did you, sir?'

'I am not yet six and thirty,' he returned.

'Oh.' She blushed at her lack of tact, but he merely smiled, taking her arm to guide her over some broken cobblestones to where an old woman perched with a large basket of flowers at her feet.

'Blossoms for your sweetheart, sir?' Spying a likely customer the woman held up roses.

Ralph Aston bought two roses and a small bunch of rosemary, a proceeding that Diana found very odd for his own garden had been richly stocked.

As they turned in at high gates, however, he said, 'My lady wife does not care to have her borders plundered. This is the chantry where Mistress Dorothy is laid. I paid for five years of masses for her soul, and her headstone is a very fine one.'

They went into the small dark church with its narrow stained glass windows and rows of tombs set into the walls.

Ralph Aston, his greying head bowed and an expression of gentle melancholy on his face, went ahead of her, the flowers in his hand. Diana, sensing that her presence at this moment might be an intrusion, turned into a side aisle where candles illumined the niches into which small memorial tablets were set. At the end of the aisle where it widened into an arched chapel graced by a statue of the Virgin, a lady knelt in prayer.

Diana paused, caught by a sense of familiarity, stepping into an alcove between two pillars as she strained her eyes towards the kneeling figure. Surely that was her mother, veiled in black, her hands clasped over her rosary. What could she possibly be doing all by herself in this strange church puzzled the girl, yet something held her back from showing herself.

Mistress Maundy rose at last, genuflected, and came slowly down the aisle, her head bent. Then she passed into the main body of the church and was lost to view.

Diana emerged from her concealment and went up towards the altar. On a small brass plaque below the rail lay a spray of white rosebuds, flowers delicate against ghostlike green foliage. She took a candle from its spike and held it close to the inscription.

'Alice Maundy.'
'1377–1381.'

A child called Alice, born in the year of Diana's own birth, dying when the Maundys had been in London. Little Alice, of whom Dame Marjorie had spoken and whom the lacemaker remembered. Little Alice, of whom nobody had ever spoken save by accident.

Trembling. she set the candle back on its

spike and went to where Ralph Aston was on his way from his devotions. There was no sign of her mother, and he seemed not to notice her own pallor.

'Mistress Dorothy was always very fond of this chantry,' he said, dropping some coins into the the alms box as they came out into the daylight again. 'She used to bring me here when I was a boy. I must take you to Temple Bar now and then hurry back to Cheapside. My wife is not happy if she has to spend too much time in the shop. She is apt to worry if many customers come in at once.'

'The house is not far now, just in the next street,' Diana said. 'I will be perfectly all right.'

'If you are certain.' He allowed himself a look of relief 'You will visit us again, my dear? You must bring your lady mother to meet us.'

'Yes, of course.' She shook hands politely and watched him hurry away, his duty discharged, care settling over him again like an extra cloak.

She walked forward slowly, her own face tight with concern. The secret she had first heard about in the peace and security of her home loomed so large now that the pleasure of her visit to the Tower was obscured.

Her mother might not yet be home. Realising this Diana lingered for a few minutes, before turning into the alley that led to the Darcy house.

She had evidently timed her arrival well, for when she tapped at the door her mother opened it at once. The veil she had worn hung with her cloak on its peg.

'I went out for a short walk. You must have just missed me,' she said, a shade of embarrassment in her tone. 'Surely you haven't come home by yourself!'

'Master Aston, Enid's father, brought me, but he had to hurry back to his shop.'

'And did you have a pleasant time? Did you see the lions at the Tower?'

'The stuffed elephant too.' Diana unfastened her cloak, recounting the events of the day in lively fashion as she thrust the episode at the chantry at the back of her mind. 'I was afraid in the boat for we went so fast and the water is so deep, but Master Todmore was very kind. Enid and Giles are most pleasant companions, and we saw everything that the public is allowed to see within the Tower. And then we walked to Cheapside where Mistress Aston prepared us a meal, and Master Aston walked the rest of the way back with me.'

'Your father went out hours ago to buy

81

tokens for the banquet at Westminster next week,' her mother said. 'You will be able to wear your best new gown, and I'll wager that you will certainly be asked to dance. That is, if he's remembered to buy tokens and not been sidetracked into some cockpit or tavern!'

'Slandering me again?' William Maundy enquired amiably from the door. 'Have a care lest I clap you into a scold's bridle!'

'I would love to see you try,' his wife retorted. 'Did you get the tokens?'

'Three of them, for a beggering sum! And I did turn aside into a tavern, my love, simply to rest my feet.'

'Which is why your breath smells of ale, I suppose,' Mistress Maundy said. 'Diana, love, go into the garden and call Jane. She has been lazing away the entire afternoon and I need her now to help me prepare supper.'

Diana went obediently, wondering if her parents would begin to talk privately when she was out of earshot, or whether her mother would keep her visit to the chantry a secret from her father too.

It was while they were eating supper that William Maundy, stabbing a piece of capon with his dagger, said, 'I forget to tell you! I made a new acquaintance when I was in the tavern. Very handsome gentleman too, in the prime of life. In fact he was buying some lavender at the corner of the street when I first went out, and we met up later in the tavern. Chance is an odd thing!'

'Very odd,' Diana muttered, and turned it into a cough when her mother glanced at her.

'Just back from France,' William said. 'He is something of an adventurer, I think, but he said he has a small castle in Kent, at a place called Marie Regina. I gained the impression that he has made his fortune and is come home to settle down.'

'Did this paragon have a name?' Kate enquired.

'Sir Godwin de Faucon. 'Tis a noble name,' he said.

' 'De' indicates noble birth, does it not?' she asked.

'Yes, indeed, though he said he was only of minor rank, but he spoke well and impressively.'

'He certainly seems to have impressed you,' Kate said.

'He had an air about him,' he admitted. 'He talked of battles and tournaments — in his youth he was in the service of the Black Prince at the Gascon Court. I told him where we were staying and he said he would make so bold as to call on us in a day or two. You will make him welcome, my love?'

'Have I ever made anyone unwelcome?' his wife demanded.

'You are the most hospitable of women,' he said promptly.

'And shall be happy to meet this Godwin de Faucon. Is he connected with the Court now?'

'I believe he has the entrée, but I gained the impression that he likes to be his own man. He told me that he has no family, and being now past forty sometimes feels lonely. I sympathize with that, for I know how I would feel without wife or loved ones.'

'Tush, go along!' Kate said, but she looked pleased.

Diana, sitting demurely in her place, felt a quiver of excitement along her nerves. She was quite certain that the Godwin de Faucon who had introduced himself to her father was the same knight who had come to her rescue in the market place and been at the Tower that morning. She was equally certain that his meeting with her father had been no accident.

'And what have you been doing with yourself all day?' William was asking.

She started slightly and then launched into an account of the Astons, carefully refraining

84

from any mention of the visit to the chantry. She had the feeling that her parents would talk of it later when she was in bed, just as they talked over so many things that she was not supposed to know.

It occurred to her, as she remembered the way the knight had looked at her, that now she had a small secret of her own.

5

Three days passed before the knight came calling, and Diana, though she refused to admit it even to herself, had begun to fear that he had no intention of coming. It was not that she found him vastly attractive but it flattered her youthful vanity to think that he was fascinated by her. Now it looked as if she had been under an illusion.

'He has likely forgotten all about it,' she said somewhat crossly to her mother as they sat together in the garden. The fine spring day made her feel restless and the boats sailing up and down the river awoke in her the desire to go somewhere and fling down the cap she was embroidering.

'A knight out of France probably has many friends to see,' Kate agreed. 'Yes, Jane, what is it?'

'A gentleman to see you, mistress,' Jane said, hovering at the back door like an anxious little hen. The maidservant had already decided that city life was too confined and too bewildering, and that she would be thankful when they all went home again.

'Then show him in,' Kate said. 'No, bring

86

him through and then fetch some wine. Did you enquire his name?'

'Godwin de Faucon, Mistress Maundy. I took the liberty of walking through.' He had moved Jane politely but firmly aside and now strode forward, hand outstretched cordially, bronze cloak swinging from his broad shoulders.

'Sir Godwin.' Kate had risen in a fluster. 'My husband is not here, I'm afraid.'

'I ought to have sent word of my coming but chance found me in your neighbourhood again.' He bowed over her hand in a manner that made her more flustered than ever.

'We never stand on ceremony, sir, but then I fear we have country ways. Jane, the wine! Bring it out here.'

'I like country ways,' he said, accepting a place next to her on the bench. 'I was reared in the depths of the country, a place called Marie Regina in Kent. I have often thought of returning to oversee my property there.'

'William said you had a castle.'

'No more than a Keep,' he disclaimed modestly. 'But you and your daughter would love the fields and woods about it.'

'Lord! I have not yet presented Diana,' Kate said flushing. 'You will think that I have no manners at all.'

'Mistress Diana and I have met,' he said.

'Her purse was taken when she was marketing and I had the great good fortune to be able to be of service.'

'Then you were the knight she spoke about,' Kate said. 'Chance is indeed a strange thing. Ah, here is the wine! You will have some, Sir Godwin?'

'Indeed I will! These dusty streets give one an inordinate thirst.'

'But it must have been worse when you were on campaign,' Kate said.'

'True, Mistress Maundy. My father was in the service of the Black Prince in Gascony, and I joined him there when I was fourteen. By the time I was twenty I'd marched more leagues than many twice my age.'

'Your father was French?'

'Aye, mistress. He was taken prisoner at Neville's Cross back in thirteen forty-six and stayed over here to acquire land. He married a Kentish girl, but my mother died in the plague when I was a lad, and after that my father and I went into France again.'

'So now you have no family?' She gave him a sympathetic look.

'I've a twin sister somewhere or other,' he said, 'but we were never close and this is my first visit to England in more than twenty years. I have a mind to settle here, for I am past forty and a man cannot wander for ever.'

'Will you go back to Kent?' Diana asked.

'One day perhaps, I've leased a house over at Chelsea for a year or two, but the country does lure me.'

'We are staying here for two or three months,' Kate informed him. 'Our home is in Devonshire, near Exeter, but we came on a visit to the city so that Diana might see a little social life.'

'It was no more than your duty, mistress,' he said. 'Such beauty ought not to be hidden from the public view. It is seldom I have the opportunity of admiring two comely ladies in one day.'

'I see that you learned how to flatter as well as to fight,' Kate said, not ill-pleased.

'I speak the truth, mistress.'

'And you will be attending the Westminster banquet?' she asked.

'Not this forthcoming one. I have business at Windsor this next week or two. But when I return I hope I shall have permission to visit you, perhaps to escort you to some place of interest?'

'Why, that would be most kind of you, sir,' Kate said. 'My husband and I have not visited London for many years and we have very few acquaintances here.'

'I have few myself,' he regretted, 'but I hope I may count you both as friends? Master Maundy too.'

'You must stay and have supper with us,' Kate invited. 'William will be home again in an hour.'

'On another occasion. I have another engagement this evening. Indeed I ought to be on my way now, but I could not resist calling in to pay my respects to you.'

'And we are happy to have met you, sir.' She clasped hands warmly as he rose. Diana, scrambling up to curtesy, felt her own hand taken in a rough clasp and was aware of his blue eyes smiling into hers. The wings of grey in his light hair gave him a look of distinction and there were lines of experience in his square, high-coloured face that interested her.

'I have not paid you for the ginger yet,' she said shyly.

'I hope you will consider that as a gift, mistress,' he said gravely.

'Then I thank you.'

Aware that her own eyes were smiling back in a glance that lingered into intimacy she dropped her gaze and bent to pick up her discarded sewing.

Her mother was walking up to the house, with Godwin de Faucon listening attentively to whatever Kate was saying. Diana, sewing in her hands, sat down on the bench and watched them go. For some reason her heart was beating jerkily, and there were beads of sweat along her hairline. Yet there was no reason in the world for her to be afraid. He was a charming and attractive gentleman, an interesting one who was obviously eager to make closer acquaintance with her. Yet for some reason it was hard to catch her breath.

'Such a gallant gentleman!' said Kate returning. 'I believe he is quite taken with you, my love. He said he would be coming to see your father on a private matter when he returned from Windsor.'

'And next week we will be at Westminster ourselves,' Diana said.

'To dine and dance,' her mother agreed, 'but you must not be too disappointed if nothing comes of it. One cannot expect anyone of higher rank than knight to interest themselves in the daughter of a farmer.'

'So we did come husband hunting,' Diana said.

'When your father dies — and we pray that won't be for many years — but when he does, the farm will revert to his second cousin,' Kate said. 'I understand provision will be made for me to stay on if I choose, but you will want to have a home of your own, a husband and children. It is what we want for you, my love.'

Diana said nothing. The feeling that she wished to find out what she wanted for herself without being told was too vague as yet for her to define. With an effort she forced herself to listen as Kate began to plan the advisability of having another gown made for her.

She was to wear the new gown of blue and silver for the banquet and the silver coif embroidered with pearls. The dress with its high waist and trailing sleeves made her look tall and stately, and her yellow hair fell in thick ringlets from beneath the demure headdress.

They had hired escorts for the ride to Westminster because it was foolhardy to venture into the city streets without protection. Peter Todmore, who came for nuncheon on the day before the banquet, declared that lawlessness had never been so bad. High prices and a scarcity of fresh meat had led to riots in several parts of the city, and the wars were going badly with more and more land being ceded to the French.

'And the Court split between those loyal to King Richard and those who favour Henry of Bolingbroke! These are dangerous times.'

'But exciting ones,' said Diana. The prospect of actually going to Court made her feel a little reckless. Perhaps some gentleman of higher rank than a knight would see her and desire her, or one of the duchesses offer her some lucrative position.

Westminster was a sprawling puzzle of a palace with so many gates and staircases, yards, towers, archways and gardens that Diana was certain they would have been completely lost if guards in royal livery had not lined the way. Their horses were taken by a groom, and their tokens by an immensely tall knight who looked down his nose at them as he waved them on into the inner courtyard.

'There are hundreds of people here,' Diana whispered, clinging to her father's arm as they passed along beneath an ornate canopy into a great apartment whose gilded ceiling stretched into shadowy recesses where halberdiers in glinting armour stood stiffly to attention.

Tables covered with white cloths and laid with dishes of silver and gilt were placed about three sides of the room. In a gallery above musicians were playing softly, and a young girl in a red dress was dancing in and out of garlands of flowers hung from the staircase. People were already scrambling for the best places at the tables, and heralds with white staves were barring the high table where the royal family were to sit.

William pushed his way to a space below the main table and helped his companions to sit at each side of him. The table glittered with ivory handledives and gilt spoons, crystal goblets and dishes of painted china. Servants were bringing in steaming bowls of meat and fish and vegetables, bright quivering jellies, candied fruits, raised pies, cakes fashioned into hearts and strewn with rose petals. Others were carrying pitchers of wine and ale. There was chatter and laughter all around them, and a bewilderment of strange faces. Diana, who had been hungry, found herself more interested in the elaborate costumes of the other guests.

Her own pretty dress paled into nothingness beside the fantastic styles worn by some of the young women. With eyebrows shaved and hair padded out over rolls of silk, their cheeks and lips rouged, they wore parti-coloured gowns with sleeves that trailed onto the ground and horned headdresses from which veils of lace and silk floated like the wings of great butterflies. Some of the men were even more elaborately garbed, the points of their shoes tied with golden chains to their low slung belts, their sleeves puffed and slashed, their hair twined with ribbons.

Somewhere beyond the hall came the clash of steel and the shrilling of trumpets. The great, iron-studded doors at the back of the apartment were flung open, and the king entered.

Now Diana saw him more closely than she had seen him when he was in the royal barge. He was tall and slim, his face long and pale, his red-gold hair waving to his shoulders below the glinting crown. His short, furred tunic was sewn with garnets and crystals, and four pages in cloth of silver held up the edges of his purple cloak with its design of lilies and leopards. Behind the monarch clustered lords and ladies adazzle with jewels, fur cloaks slipping carelessly from their shoulders, their heads raised so high that she suspected their necks must ache.

'That is the king's cousin, Henry of Bolingbroke,' her father whispered.

She followed his pointing knife to the burly courtier with red hair cut shorter than the prevailing fashion and a look of settled pugnacity on his face.

'He looks like a soldier,' she said.

'He's been in many campaigns,' he told her, 'and he's the whip hand over most of the nobles. Only his father's influence prevents him from reaching now for the throne.'

'You should not speak so freely,' she said nervously.

'Tush! There's nobody to pay heed. There is little Lord Harry, who is Bolingbroke's son, grandson to Lancaster.'

'He seems fond of the king,' she said, watching the lad perch on the king's knee, seeing the elegant, heavily ringed hand smooth the boy's hair and the haughty face soften into a half-smile.

'The king is fond of children, they say,' Kate interposed. 'It is sad that he and the late queen had none of their own.'

The food was being eaten now, the wines drunk, and a tumbler was flipping over and over, a ball between his feet.

'There are the king's uncles,' William pointed. 'John of Gaunt is a fine looking man, don't you think?'

Diana, her mouth full of carp, nodded. The Duke of Lancaster wore a long gown of emerald and there were diamonds sewn in apparent confusion over the sleeves. In contrast his brothers, Edmund of York and Thomas of Gloucester, were clad in dark robes barred with ermine. They were small, thin, dark men who stared frowningly at everybody else and drank their wine in quick, nervous gulps.

It was strange, she thought, that these three

dukes were all sons of the mighty Edward the Third and that Edward's crown should have descended to his grandson, the proud young man who sat now, with his cousin's son upon his knee, and gazed about him as if the scene bored him exceedingly.

A herald, scarlet sleeves brushing the floor, was moving up and down the tables, presenting small copper disks apparently at random.

'Those who receive one will be allowed to approach His Grace,' William said. 'Only twenty or thirty are given out at each public banquet, so you may imagine they are highly prized.'

Diana guessed that the herald would probably have been bribed, but she could not resist throwing him an imploring look as he approached, and to her surprise he hesitated, then gave her one.

'My love, you will meet the king!' Kate exclaimed, her round face crimsoning with pleasure. 'Oh, but this is a stroke of good fortune!'

'Remember to give your name clearly,' William instructed fussily.

'And to make your curtsey as you have been taught,' Kate added.

'Yes, of course.' She gave them the patient smile of an adult irritated by the vapourings of children, and clutched the token firmly.

The king was rising, the pages scurrying to lift his heavy robe. As far as Diana could tell he had drunk some wine and nibbled on a candied fruit. She wondered if he disliked having to eat in front of people who had paid for the privilege of watching him.

The tables were being cleared and moved, with the benches to the side of the room. An anxious looking official was counting spoons and another was marshalling those with copper tokens into a line. The trumpets sounded again as the royal party withdrew, and in the gallery the musicians began to play a round dance.

'This way.' One of the attendants tapped Diana on the shoulder and she followed him out of the hall and down a short passage into an ornately gilded chamber with a dais at one end. The king sat upon it, and as she approached she saw again the boredom on the pale face, the slight curl of the lip above the pointed beard.

She sank into the most graceful curtsey she could manage and heard her own voice, pitched a little high.

'Mistress Diana Maundy, Your Grace.'

'From which part of the country?' he asked.

'Out of Devonshire, Your Grace.'

'She's comely, with unpocked skin,' the king remarked, motioning her to rise.

'And of good family, judging from her bearing,' one of the other courtiers said.

'And you, cousin Mowbray, are an expert on breeding,' the king remarked, his smile down slanting. 'Are you married yet, Mistress Maundy?'

'No, Your Grace.'

'The men in Devonshire must be blind,' the Duke of Lancaster said. He was staring at Diana with the frank appreciation of a lusty man for a pretty maid.

'Are you thinking of taking another mistress now that you are wed to your last one?' Thomas of Gloucester enquired.

'With Katharine as my wife I need no other woman,' John of Gaunt said. 'The case may be different with you, brother.'

'Have you any petition for us?' The king bestowed a cold glance at his relatives and addressed himself to Diana.

'I wished to convey my regards to Maudelyn Falcon,' she ventured.

'Maudelyn? Do we know the gentleman?' he enquired.

'Maudelyn is a son of mine,' the Duke of Lancaster said.

'One of your bastards?' Edmund of York smiled, his lips thinning.

'The only one, since His Grace gave me leave to wed Mistress Swynford and so legitimise my Beaufort family,' the Duke said blandly. 'So you know my lad, do you?'

'I met him once, sir,' she said shyly.

'Only once. He must have made a considerable impression on you in a very short time!'

'He was passing through, sir, and we talked for a few minutes,' she confided. 'He said that if ever I came to Court I was to ask for him.'

'Your son seems to have inherited some of your qualities, uncle,' the king remarked. 'Let us hope that we don't have a constant succession of young women descending upon us from every corner of the kingdom.'

'Maudelyn is in my castle of Kenilworth,' the Duke said. 'I will tell him, when I next see him, that Mistress Diana Maundy wishes to be remembered to him.'

He spoke kindly, but there was amusement in his eyes.

'I am obliged to you, my lord,' she said stiffly.

'And you are not wed? You must be past seventeen!' the king said.

'Yes, Your Grace.'

'Have your parents any plans for you?' the Duke asked.

'I believe they have, sir, but they will not force me to anything,' she said.

'And you have sufficient dowry?'

'I believe so, sir,'

'Give the wench a trinket,' the king ordered. 'She has asked for nothing, therefore it pleases us to give her something.'

He clicked his fingers and a page, carrying a small basket, came forward and knelt.

'Choose a jewel,' the king said. 'There are some pretty pearls there and some rubies.'

'The wench should have a blue stone,' said the Duke of Lancaster, stepping from the dais and plunging his own fingers in. 'Here's a sapphire clasp to wear in your hair. That will suit you best, for it darkens your eyes to the same shade.'

'I thank Your Grace.' She included both king and duke in her smile.

'We wish you good fortune, mistress,' the king said in dismissal.

She backed away until one of the guards touched her arm, indicating the door that would take her back into the main hall. The audience was over and already another lady was kneeling before the dais.

Her parents were waiting for her, their faces tense and excited.

'Did His Grace speak to you?' Kate asked.

'He asked my name and where I came

from,' Diana said. 'The Duke of Lancaster spoke to me too. And the king gave me this. The duke picked it out for me though.'

'It's beautiful!' Kate clasped her hands. 'Let me put it into your coif for you. 'Tis a very pretty colour.'

'And a fair sized stone,' William judged. 'His Grace is generous.'

The other people were all dancing, or mingling in small groups as the men servants circulated with more wine. The music was fast and furious, the dancers leaping and twisting, joining hands, then breaking free again to skip in time to the music.

A young gallant, his tunic sewn with flowers, came up to request Diana's hand in the measure. Fortunately it was a dance she knew and not one of the elaborate Court ones, and she kept time with ease, earning several glances of admiration from some young knights standing in the corner.

She was whirled on, another man partnering her. One or two of the royal party had returned and were watching, goblets in their hands. She caught a glimpse of the one they had called Mowbray, and then a gentleman with lank fair hair was leading her onto the floor again.

The torches had been lit and flared in their sconces, casting flickering shadows over the walls and floor. In some parts of the hall stools had been placed for those who were past the age of dancing, and several black robed matrons leaned their heads together, whispering as the younglings danced past.

'My dear, it is time we were leaving.' Her father was touching her on the arm.

'Must we go now?' She cast a wistful look at the others.

'The gates are opened at twelve and those who have not paid are allowed in to eat what is left over,' William said. 'It would be much wiser to leave.'

'Very well, my love,' Kate said at once. She had enjoyed the evening immensely, she had even danced twice, but her feet were beginning to ache and there was the prospect of the long ride home through the dark streets.

They made their way out into the courtyard and waited, shivering in the night air, as their mounts were brought and their hired escorts routed out of the kitchens where they had been eating a more plebian supper.

Out of the shadows a cloaked figure stepped, detaining her briefly.

'You're the wench who sent her regards to my lad?'

'Yes, my lord.'

'You're a comely lass,' the Duke said. 'I

hope you're a sensible one, too.'

'I try to be, sir.'

'Then find yourself a good man and wed him with your parents' blessing,' he advised. 'Maudelyn is a bird of passage and such are not the stuff of which good husbands are made. I wish you joy for your future, child.'

He had spoken low and now he raised her hand to his lips and was gone into the darkness again, as her father called to her,

'Come along, Diana! At this rate it will be morning before we reach Temple Bar again!'

6

'My dear, do you like Sir Godwin de Faucon?' Kate questioned.

'What I know of him,' Diana said cautiously.

'He has been most attentive since his return from Windsor,' her mother said. 'Hardly a day has passed but he has called to pay his respects.'

'And on the days he misses father rushes out to meet him at the cockpit or the tavern,' Diana agreed.

'You have such an odd note in your voice,' Kate complained mildly. 'I hope you are not becoming weary with city life.'

'I enjoy it,' Diana assured her, 'but I wish — this is so hard to try to explain, but I wish I could have a little time to think.'

'To think about what?'

'About what I want to do,' Diana said.

'What's to think about?' Kate asked in bewilderment. 'You want to be married and have a home of your own, don't you?'

'Yes. Yes, I think I do.'

'You've not got it into your head that you want to enter the religious life, have you?'

Kate enquired. 'If that is in your mind, I won't deny it'd be a disappointment, but we'd not stop you.'

'I'd hate to be a nun,' Diana said firmly. 'It's simply that I want time to find out about myself.'

'There's nothing to find,' Kate said sharply. 'You are our dear daughter, William's and mine, and we want the best we can provide for you.'

'Like Godwin de Faucon?' Diana muttered under her breath as she turned aside.

He would be here again for supper tonight. Recently he had been to see them nearly every day, and under his guidance they had explored much of the city. He was very genial and well-mannered, she considered, with an air of experience that obviously interested her parents, and a way of phrasing a delicate compliment that pleased her. Yet something within her held back from him and she could not have told why.

'Do you mind if I go out for a little while?' she asked. 'I'll not go far, but I need some air.'

'You'll not be long?'

'I promise.' She bestowed a quick reassuring kiss on her mother, took her cloak from the peg, and went out into the street.

They had been nearly seven weeks in

London and she sensed that soon her parents would be asking for some decision from her. She knew too, though they had never reminded her of it, that they had spent a lot of money in order to bring her to the city. She had not been offered a place at Court, but a knight was paying her undoubted attentions and it was ungrateful of her to hesitate.

Without realising it she had walked to the high gates which led to the little, dark chantry, where she had seen her mother kneeling. The flower seller was not here today, but the gates stood open and, hesitating, she passed within.

A priest, sweeping pebbles from the path, stood aside as she paused at the door and spoke cordially.

'Good morrow, child. Was it help you seek or do you merely visit?'

'I came to visit,' she said.

'But it is dark and silent within, eh?' Misunderstanding her hesitation he set his broom against the outer wall and spoke kindly, 'You must not fear the dead. Their souls are in heaven and only their bones lie here. Is it a relative who is buried here?'

'A — distant one,' she said slowly. 'Alice Maundy. She died at four, thirteen years ago. I wondered how she died.'

'Her name will be in the register, together with the cause of death. If you wish, I can show it to you,' he offered.

'That would be very kind of you,' she said gratefully.

'The registers are in the sacristy,' he informed her. 'We pride ourselves on keeping them very carefully. Watch the step for it is dark within.'

She followed him obediently, lifting her skirts clear of the step as he pattered ahead of her down the gloomy aisle.

The heavily bound ledgers were piled neatly on glass fronted shelves.

'Seven years in each volume,' he said, panting as he lifted one down. 'Thirteen years, did you say?'

'Thirteen eighty-one.'

'Then it's fourteen years. You don't know the date, I suppose?'

'It was in the month that the peasants rose up under Wat Tyler.'

'Ah, in summer then. That was a terrible time. The Archbishop had his head struck off, you know, and many went in fear of their lives. Alice Maundy you said, now let me see.'

He turned the pages with irritating slowness, running his finger down the columns.

'Maunch, Maunchey, Maundy. Here it

is! '8th June, 1381. Alice Maundy, aged four years of Devonshire. Cause of death smallpox.' '

'May I see?' She took the book and read the entry for herself.

'Her parents left gold for a memorial and for a year's masses. So young a child would not have needed more. Was that what you wished to see?'

'Thank you, yes.' She smiled at the priest as she turned to leave, but there was a sick, cold feeling inside her and her hands were clammy.

'The death of a child is always a sad affair,' the priest said. 'We must remember however that the good Lord knows best.'

'I wonder sometimes if He does,' Diana said, and leaving the priest staring at her with a shocked expression on his face, hurried out of the chantry.

So there really had been a child called Alice. A sister? But in that case why had she never been told about her? Surely the death of a sister was not something to be kept secret!

She walked on restlessly, ignoring the jostling of passers by and the seductive cries of the street hawkers. She was not looking where she was going, and the exasperated comments of a stallholder into whose produce she inadvertently banged passed over her head.

'Mistress! If you walk with such lack of care you will soon be run over or injured!' a voice cried, laughing.

She came back from a great distance and stood, mouth agape, staring at him.

'You have not forgotten me, have you?' he was asking. 'My father told me that you wished to be remembered to me.'

'No. No, of course I have not.' She was stammering a little.

'And I find you, not at Court, but wandering alone in the middle of the city! Come, we'll take the weight off our feet in a tavern. You'll not object to having a drink with me?'

She had never been in a tavern in her life but she nodded eagerly and went with him through the narrow doorway into the rush strewn chamber with its benches and tables. 'You'll have ale or wine?' he questioned, showing her to a seat.

'Wine please.' She clasped her hands together to still their trembling and watched him as he went up to the railed corner where the tavern keeper stood. He had not changed since their brief meeting in the church. His lank yellow hair, his narrow brilliantly green eyes, his elegantly clad frame, roused in her feelings that had lain dormant for months.

'So!' He returned with two brimming goblets. 'You came to London after all. My father told me that you were at the public banquet.'

'My father bought tokens,' she said.

'I wish I had been there. I'd have ensured no other gallant had the opportunity of dancing with you. What think you of the king?'

'He looks very proud,' she said cautiously, 'and very lonely. He looks as if he does not like showing himself in public.'

'My father supports him through thick and thin,' Maudelyn said. 'He has little cause to fear for his throne while Lancaster lives.'

'But the other dukes — '

'Snarl like dogs waiting under the table for bones. Edmund of York is not much of a problem for he has few friends and little power. Thomas of Gloucester has the worst temper of any man I ever met, but he is friend to Mowbray, and Mowbray has ambitions.'

'And you? Do you have ambitions too?' she asked.

'To make my fortune and be free as the wind,' he said promptly.

'Oh.' She dropped her gaze, fiddling with the goblet, disappointment flooding through her.

111

'A bastard must make his own way in the world,' Maudelyn said. 'My father taught me that. He gave me a knightly training and a fair allowance and freedom to make up my own mind. No son could expect more.'

She would have liked to ask about his mother but feared to embarrass him. Instead she said, 'And you have made up your mind to be free?'

'Until I can no longer avoid it,' he said. 'I've travelled much in France and Spain. My father trusts me to carry messages — important ones too, some of them.'

He was boasting a little, but she was young enough to share his pleasure in his own achievement, and she laughed with him though disappointment still ran through her.

'The duke is wed again, is he not?,' she said.

'To Katharine Swynford,' he nodded. 'She is one of the sweetest ladies I ever met. You know, the duke would have wed her many years ago but his Spanish wife was still alive. It is to her credit that she remained loyal to him, and he to her during so many years.'

'You are fond of her too,' she said.

'Very fond. She was always good to me, as if I were one of her own. She never grudged my being at Kenilworth, never once showed any trace of jealousy. A lady through to her bones.'

A little dart of jealousy shot through Diana and was as quickly suppressed.

'And you have never thought of marrying?' she ventured.

'Not until I've seen everything that I want to see, and made my fortune,' he said gaily. 'Do you know any maid who'd wait so long?'

'Maids like to be wed,' she said in a low voice.

'True.' He gave a rueful grin as he drained the last of his wine. 'Now, tell me of yourself. How long will you be in the city?'

'Another month, I believe.'

'I have often thought of our meeting in that tiny church,' he said. 'Friends can meet in such strange ways, have you noticed? And meet seldom, yet still remain friends? I'd swear that if we were to part now and chance upon each other in ten years time the ease of old acquaintenship would still be with us!'

'Yes,' she said, her heart sinking. 'Are you — are you going away soon?'

'I hope so. I've nothing to delay me in London now that the plague season will soon be upon us. I've a fancy to go to Ireland, you know. There are savage tribes there who play

113

upon harps and still worship strange gods.'

'Will you be gone for a long time?' she asked.

'A year or two. I dislike having to plan too far ahead.'

'Yes, of course.' She raised her chin slightly smiling.

'When I come back, with a pocketful of Irish gold, will you welcome me as a friend?' he asked smiling back.

'Yes, of course,' she said lightly.

'Then we'll make a bargain.' He leaned across, clasping her hand in his. 'I will come back in a year or two and we will weave again the threads of our friendship. Shall we agree on that?'

She remembered the kindness in the Duke of Lancaster's quiet voice when he had told her that Maudelyn was a bird of passage, and she would do well to find herself a husband. He had been right, but it gave her no pleasure.

'Agreed,' she said aloud.

'And I have no more time.' He rose, regret in his face. 'My half-brother John is at the Savoy and I am engaged for supper with him. I'll walk back with you.'

'No need. This part of the city is quite safe during the day. I am becoming quite a Londoner, you see.'

'With that skin and hair? The country bred those,' he said gracefully.

'And I wish you Godspeed,' she said, her breath catching in her throat because this meeting too had been so brief and so fruitless. He was heart free and she lacked the wiles to trap him.

'As I do you, Mistress Diana.' He raised his hand and was gone, striding out into the crowds without a backward glance.

'Did you want anything else?' the tavern keeper asked loudly from the corner.

'Nothing.' Aware that his tone suggested that she was a drab, she rose pulling her cloak about her and went out with as much dignity as she could muster.

Finding her way back to Temple Bar was easy, for the streets were indeed becoming more familiar to her, but she was still not happy to look up at a sky obscured by smoke. At this season the countryside around her home would be beautiful, the cows knee deep in buttercups and clover, the birds feeding their young in the nests they had built under the eaves.

When she passed the gates leading to the church she averted her head slightly, not wanting to think about the entry in the register or about the memorial plaque where her mother had laid the rosebuds.

Kate greeted her with agitation in her face and voice.

'A short walk indeed! It has lasted over two hours! Where in the world have you been?'

'Just walking. I told you that I wanted to think.'

'Then I trust you thought to good purpose,' Kate said irritably, 'for your father will be here at any moment with Sir Godwin, and you still have on your plain gown. Come upstairs and I'll help you to change. And try to pinch some colour into your face. Your walk has made you very pale.'

Diana went obediently upstairs where her mother commenced to fuss about, taking out first one dress and then another.

'For I really cannot make up my mind which is more suitable for a quiet evening at home.'

'My russet gown,' Diana said promptly.

'You are grown tiresomely provoking these past weeks,' Kate complained.

'Sir Godwin has seen me in my russet gown before. Why is this evening so different?'

'Because he has made it clear that he intends to ask for your hand,' Kate confided. 'And there is no need to flush and twitch in that fashion. We have known for days that he would ask.'

'Then why must I get dressed up as if we

were going to a Court banquet again?'

'Because this is to be a happy occasion.'

'So I am to accept him?'

'My love, we should never have encouraged his visits, if we had not favoured his suit,' Kate said, shocked. 'He is a very well-set up gentleman, dear, a knight of good family who has made sufficient money to settle down and found a family.'

'I like him well.' Diana's voice was muffled as her mother thrust the blue gown over her head. 'He is much older than I am.'

'Not many years past forty, and he does not look his age. A mature man makes a better husband than a callow lad. And it is not as if you were in love with anyone else. You are not, are you?'

Anxiety crept into her voice as she gazed at her daughter.

'You are not, are you?' she repeated.

'There was a young man who passed through last summer,' Diana said slowly. 'A young man called Maudelyn Falcon.'

'The one who stopped by at Father Anthony's? The Duke of Lancaster's bastard?'

'He was a fine young man,' Diana said wistfully. Kate was silent for a moment, her face very still. When she spoke next her voice was gentle.

'When I was a maid there was a squire lived

in the next village. Eyes blue as cornflowers he had and shoulders like an ox. He danced with me once at Yuletide and he held me as if I were beautiful. He made me feel beautiful did that young man, and I never was beautiful, you know. And then my father told me that he had handfasted me to William Maundy and we were to be married in the summer. I cried a little that night, and I dreamed that perhaps the young squire would carry me off and wed me secretly. It never happened of course. I wed your father, and I learned to love him very much. Few wives have been as fortunate as I have been.'

'And the young squire? What happened to him?

'Why, I suppose he married someone else,' Kate said. 'William and I moved away, you see, and made our home together, and it would have been disloyal to have thought about another man. All girls have dreams, my lovely, but the time comes when we must lay dreams aside.'

'I saw Maudelyn Falcon again today,' Diana said.

'Oh?' Kate frowned slighty.

'He remembered me. I ran into him by chance, and he remembered me.'

'Did he speak of love?'

'He spoke of friendship,' Diana said

reluctantly. 'He is going to Ireland, he says, to make his fortune.'

'But he did not speak of love?'

Diana shook her head, tears rushing into her eyes.

'It's best that he should go and that you should forget him,' Kate said. 'You're a dear, good child, and your father and I want only the best for you. We came to London for that purpose.'

'You hoped I'd get a position at Court,' Diana said.

'Ah, it was only a little hope!' Kate said smilingly. 'I have always wanted you to be settled and wed.'

'To Sir Godwin de Faucon?'

'He has a castle in Kent, and he is considering a return to his home. You would be happier in the country than in the town, wouldn't you?'

'I think so.'

'Not that Sir Godwin would bury you in the countryside,' Kate assured her. 'I am certain that he will bring you often to the city. There may be Court banquets that you can attend. Remember that he has the 'de' in his name which indicates nobility.'

'And he seems to be very kind,' Diana said.

Kate's face brightened. 'Very kind and

greatly taken with you. He told me that you were one of the loveliest maids he had ever seen.'

'Then you'd best help me pin up my hair,' Diana said, 'lest he have cause to change his opinion.'

Her feeble little joke cast down her spirits even further, but Kate smiled with relief. In a little while, Diana thought ruefully, she would convince herself that Maudelyn Falcon had been no more than a dream and that she loved Sir Godwin.

'Your father's home!' Kate exclaimed at the sound of voices and footsteps below. 'Put the blue clasp in your hair and follow me down in a few minutes.'

She patted the girl on the shoulder and bustled out.

Diana fastened the sapphire into the long ringlet at the side of her head, bit her lip nervously, and went slowly down to the living room.

Sir Godwin was in a long gown of dark olive velvet. It made him look more her father's contemporary than her own, and she felt a moment's shyness. Then he stepped forward, clasping her hands warmly, his eyes complimenting her.

'Godwin and I have been discussing the future,' William said. 'I have a suspicion that your lady mother has been talking to you on the same subject, eh, Diana?'

'Diana is very conscious of the honour you have paid her,' Kate said formally.

'And willing to accept, I trust?'

He smiled at her, the smile of a man who expected a pleasant answer.

'Diana has always been guided by us,' William interposed. 'As I told you she is very well educated for a female. She reads and writes in French and English and she even knows some Latin.'

'You will have him thinking she is nothing but a student,' Kate protested. 'I reared her to be a careful housewife, sir. She can bake and sew as well as I can myself, and she's healthy. She's very healthy.'

'Her dowry is the best I could gather since she was a little thing,' William said. 'We have lived modestly but comfortably for years, saving everything we could towards Diana's marriage.'

'The dowry suits me well but the lady pleases me better,' Godwin said.

'Then we'll drink to it,' William said. 'Long life and happiness to you both. I tell you frankly that it will be a weight off my mind to know that my wench is in good hands.'

'Now that it is settled, perhaps you will

allow me to take Mistress Diana into the garden for a while before supper?' Godwin said.

'Of course you may.' Kate was beaming as William opened the back door.

The shadows were long and thin across the grass but the sun was still warm and had flung a Jacob's ladder across the river.

'You are very silent,' Godwin said, glancing at her as they walked down to the boundary wall. 'I trust that you are happy, mistress.'

'My parents are pleased that I am to be wed.'

'And you? Are you pleased? I'd not have an unwilling bride.'

'I cannot tell, sir,' she said, twisting her fingers together. 'We have not talked much together.'

'Talked?' He gave her a faintly puzzled frown. 'I cannot see what talking has to do with choosing a wife.'

'You don't know much about me,' she hesitated.

'Why, what's to know? You're young, comely, healthy, and your dowry's not to be sneezed at,' he said. 'Nay, don't flush and turn aside! I was only jesting. I have never seen a maiden I liked so well, and I've been near marrying once or twice. Oh, I'm aware that I'm older than you, but I'm not yet in my dotage. I am still capable of siring a son.'

'Is that what you want?' she asked in a small voice.

'Doesn't every man? And you'd like a child too, wouldn't you? All wenches like babies.'

'Later on,' she said.

'Oh, I'll not rush you. You shall have your time to read and sew and wear pretty dresses,' he said tolerantly. 'Look, I have a betrothal ring for you. I hope I guessed the size aright.'

He had lifted her hand and was slipping a carved ring upon her finger. The emerald was square cut, set in gold, and it felt cold and heavy.

'I am going to persuade your parents to let us wed at the beginning of next month,' he said. 'Then we will go to Marie Regina, to my old home there. It is thirty years since I visited the place, and I don't doubt there is much to be done there, but the woods and fields will be the same I hope. There is a monastery there. And my sister used to spend a whole day there, poring over the manuscripts. She may still be there for all I know. It will be a surprise for her when I come back with a pretty wife. Does the ring please you?'

'Very much,' she lied. It looked clumsy

on her hand and the colour reminded her of Maudelyn's green eyes.

'Then don't I get a kiss for it?'

She held up her face and felt his hot breath on her cheek.

'I was going to kiss you,' he said, faint displeasure in his voice. 'You screw up your eyes as if you feared a bite. Are all wenches from Devonshire so cool?'

'I cannot tell.'

'No need to fret,' he said amiably. 'I'll warm you in the marriage bed.'

'Next month,' she said and thought of the narrow barred windows in the Tower and the armed guards pacing above the walls.

'A quiet wedding and a leisurely journey into Kent.' He put his arm about her and she smiled, aware of a quivering at the base of her spine though she could not have told if it was attraction or repulsion. Neither could she have told at that moment if she was happy or miserable.

7

'With the marriage in less than a month there'll be small time to get everything ready,' Kate grumbled happily.

'I wish I could be married from home, instead of in the city,' Diana said.

'There's little point in our going all the way back to Devon when you are going at once into Kent,' her mother observed. 'I think an overgown of very pale blue and a white coif would look well on you, my love. The licence has to be obtained but that is not our concern. Now as to the bride cake — '

Diana was not much interested in the subject of bride cake. She was not even much interested in the wedding, for the arrangements had all been taken out of her hands and she had the odd feeling that some other girl would stand at the church door to be joined in matrimony to Godwin de Faucon.

'We know so few people in London,' Kate frowned, 'but there are the Todmores and the Astons. To be sure I have little in common with Mistress Todmore but we must have a few guests.'

'May I go over to Cheapside and tell the Astons? I've not seen them since we visited the Tower. Why, they'll not even have heard that I am betrothed!' Diana exclaimed.

'Very well. Take Jane with you.'

'Jane's at market.'

'Then don't speak to any strangers and leave your purse at home lest it be snatched.' Kate spoke as if Diana had lost every purse she had ever owned.

'Mistress Aston will likely offer me nuncheon,' the girl said, 'so don't expect me back too soon.'

It was a fine, warm day at that moment when spring makes up its mind to be summer, but before summer itself grows dry and weary and the pestilence begins. Diana took her time, glad of the opportunity to be away from her mother's eager planning, her father's constant assertion that her dowry would be a good one.

When she reached the Aston house she paused for an instant, noting a roll of cloth in the window of a rich turquoise shade. It seemed that Giles was already persuading his father to experiment with new dyes.

'Why, it's Mistress Diana, surely!' Ralph Aston had come to the door and was staring at her.

'Yes, sir. I hope you don't mind my calling?'

'Not at all.' He shook hands cordially. 'But I'm afraid my wife and children are away for a few days. A cousin of my wife's is being wed and I gave her and the younglings leave to go to Oxford for the event. They would have called upon you before this had they been here. But come up to the living room. You shall have a nuncheon after your long walk.'

'I didn't intend to interrupt your work,' she said shyly.

'Not at all. I'll close the shop for half an hour and join you. I've been looking after myself this past week and it will be pleasant to have company.'

She went up the narrow stairs into the modestly comfortable room where Mistress Aston had entertained her before.

'There is some brawn in a pie,' Ralph Aston said, lumbering in with a tray. 'Some marchpane and sugared pears, and the wine is good. Do clear those things from the table, my dear, and we will be able to eat in a trice. Now, do let us sit down. You had best take off your cloak, or you will not feel the benefit when you go out again.'

He seemed pleased to have the opportunity to talk to someone.

'I ought to have sent word,' she apologised, 'but I have been occupied with my own affairs, and Master Todmore has been kept close to his studies these past weeks.'

'Your parents are well? I'd promised to call upon them.'

'Quite well, and very happy on my account,' she assured him. 'I am newly betrothed, sir, and to be wed in a fortnight.'

'Wed? Now that is a matter for rejoicing,' he said, looking pleased.

'I came to tell Mistress Aston and to invite you all to come. It is to be in London and we don't know many people here.'

'I shall certainly come if it be possible,' he said. 'This match is a good one, I take it? Your father and mother are satisfied?'

'Yes. Yes, they are both pleased.'

'And you too are content?' Something in her tone must have arrested his attention for he glanced at her sharply.

'He seems very kind,' she said. 'Older than I am, and much more travelled, but a goodly man.'

'And his name?'

'Godwin. Sir Godwin de Faucon, but he is retired from soldiering after many years in France.'

'Godwin?' He was in the act of passing her a slice of brawn pie but he set the dish down

128

again on the table and stared at her.

'Godwin de Faucon. The 'de' indicates nobility though he is not of a very high rank.'

'De Faucon. Godwin de Faucon.'

'As you say, sir.' Diana gazed at him in perplexity, for he repeated the name in a hoarse voice.

'You cannot wed him,' he said at last. 'You cannot possibly wed him! No innocent wench should be exposed to such a man!'

'Master Aston, why? You know him?'

'To my cost.' He stared at her as if he relived some other scene. 'Godwin de Faucon ruined my life.'

'How so?'

'It is not a tale for young ears.'

'But I am contracted to wed him,' she argued. 'Surely, if there is some reason why I ought not to marry, then I have the right to be told.'

'It's a long story,' he said reluctantly.

'I'm not expected back for a while,' she said.

'It began before I was born,' he said. 'My father was a Norfolk man, as I believe I told you. He had a friend, a man whom he admired tremendously, a French knight called Pierre de Faucon. They both married, and my father and mother settled in Cheapside. Pierre de Faucon and his wife lived at Marie Regina in Kent.'

'But Sir Godwin has a castle there!' she exclaimed.

'The castle belongs to the local monastery. Pierre de Faucon leased it, I believe. There were twins born of his marriage, Gida and Godwin. When the plague came my parents were staying at Marie Regina. They died of it and so did Alfreda, Pierre's wife. There was only Dorothy, the housekeeper, to take care of us, Gida, Godwin and me. I was a babe then.'

'So you knew him such a long time ago?'

'When he was still a lad he went to Gascony with his father and Gida obtained a position at Court. Dorothy brought me back here, to my father's shop and ran the business for me until I was of an age to take over. We saw Gida from time to time.'

'And Godwin?'

'He stayed in France after his father died. We heard nothing of him for years, and then he walked in one day, bold as you please. He could not have come at a worse moment, though I didn't know it then. I was sixteen years old and I was betrothed. It had been arranged for years and it was the most important thing in my life. The most important thing.'

'To Mistress Aston?'

'No.' He shook his head. 'I was to marry a wench called Petrella Grey. Petrella.' His voice lingered over the name.

'Was she pretty?'

'The prettiest thing you ever saw. Fifteen years old and sweet as honey. She had dark hair and a gentle face, gentle and trusting. She trusted everybody.'

'And Godwin?' She stared at him in apprehension.

'She trusted Godwin too, and he betrayed her,' Ralph Aston said and his face was tight with remembered pain. 'He had his pleasure of her and then he went back to France, leaving a babe in her. I was young and I swore I would never forgive her.'

'But if you loved her — '

'I was young,' he repeated. 'I kept the anger bright and fierce in my heart.'

'And Petrella? What happened to her?'

'Petrella ran away,' he said heavily. 'She ran away and Godwin's sister, Gida, left London at the same time. She had already borne a bastard of her own, so took small account of morals. Later on that year she sent word to Dorothy that Petrella had miscarried and died.'

'I'm sorry for it,' she said gravely.

'I have not mentioned Petrella's name

since, nor seen Gida or Godwin,' he told her. 'I married Mistress Ann Todmore and she has been the best wife a man could wish, but I swore long ago that if I ever laid eyes on Godwin again I'd kill him. And now you tell me he is in London and you are betrothed to him!'

'If it all happened so long ago,' Diana began, but he interrupted her, his voice passionate.

'I swore it! He cheated me and seduced Petrella and then deserted her. Do you think any man could forget that? I prayed that he was dead. I believed that he must have died because I had heard nothing of him in all these years.'

'He is just returned from France.'

'And where lodging?'

'In Chelsea. He has rented a house there.'

'And he has offered for your hand.'

'I met him at Smithfield Market. He helped me when my purse was stolen and later got into conversation with my father. He intends to marry and settle down in Kent. Perhaps he has changed in the years since you knew him.'

'You have an affection for him?' He looked at her with raised brows.

'An affection?' She bit her lip, frowning. 'He seems kind,' she said at last. 'My parents brought me to London in the hope of finding me a husband, and they were pleased when Sir Godwin offered for me.'

'He is no fit mate for any maid,' Ralph Aston said.

'You said you hadn't seen him for many years. He may have changed.' It was foolish but she felt obliged to defend him.

'Men like that never change,' he said coldly. 'A young man who will desert a girl he has already betrayed will not change.'

'I am sorry for it,' she said in a low voice, and wondered if the shrinking she felt when Godwin touched her was a measure of her instinctive distrust of him. Yet he had fascinated her from the beginning.

'Is that your bethrothal ring?' Ralph Aston asked. She nodded, holding out her hand for him to see it.

'It is a handsome ring,' he admitted. 'Godwin must have done well.'

'My parents wish me to be happy,' she said, sensing criticism. 'They would not marry me to a man simply for his wealth.'

'But you have no affection for him, I trust? I would not have any young wench of my acquaintance bound by affection to such a knave.'

'Master Aston, if it was so long ago then he was young too. And your sweetheart — he did not force her, did he? Was she not also to blame?'

'And paid for it,' he said, 'for she died in miscarrying of her bastard. But he still lives and is in London. Does he know that you are acquainted with me?'

'I doubt if your name has been mentioned, sir.'

'Then keep it so.' Glancing at her white face he added in a more moderate tone. 'You must try to put this from your mind and keep in confidence what I have said to you. You will give me your word on that?'

'Yes, sir.'

'And now we will eat our nuncheon and talk of other matters.'

'I am not very hungry, sir.' She looked at the brawn pie with distaste.

'Nor am I.' He gave her a slightly twisted grin and rose, the betrayed and bitter lover submerged by the merchant again. 'You understand that I could not attend this marriage, and I beg you most earnestly to reconsider.'

'I could only do that by betraying your confidence and telling my parents,' she said, 'and I doubt if it would achieve anything. They would put it down to youthful folly on Sir Godwin's part, for men are expected to be experienced.'

'Then it's best you say nothing. We shall keep this matter between ourselves. It is not a tale to be spread abroad, for a man's pain should be private.'

Diana nodded, reaching for her cloak as she rose. Ralph Aston's good humour had fled, and she guessed, from his lowering expression, that he was anxious to be alone again, no doubt to brood over the past.

'I wish that I could give you hearty congratulations,' he said, 'but I cannot. If you marry Godwin I see nothing but misery ahead for you, and I tremble at my own forebodings.'

She followed him downstairs again, her mood down-cast. It was as if his words had aroused in her all the apprehension she had tried to ignore ever since Godwin de Faucon had placed the heavy emerald ring upon her finger.

'I bid you God-speed, mistress,' he said. 'You will be safe going alone back to Temple Bar? I can send my apprentice with you.'

'I know my way well now,' she assured him.

They parted without shaking hands. It was as if, by her betrothal, Ralph Aston considered she had taken upon herself something of Godwin de Faucon's guilt. Yet, in fairness, she had to weigh against that Ralph Aston's own unforgiving nature. He had betrayed Petrella too by casting her off when he learned of her seduction. Perhaps he too had been to blame.

'The Astons are away,' she told Kate briefly on her return.

'Ah, there's a pity!' Her mother's face showed disappointment. 'Well, there are still the Todmores. You must call upon them tomorrow and give them an invitation, my love.'

'Is Sir Godwin coming to supper tonight?' Diana asked.

She was not certain she could face him, with her new found knowledge troubling her mind, and it was a relief to hear Kate say, 'Not tonight, he is staying home tonight. I understand we are to supper with him in Chelsea tomorrow. Now that the betrothal papers are signed, it will benefit your happiness to spend as much time as possible with him so that you will be able to appreciate his good qualities the more.'

She was glad of the respite, and, pleading tiredness, went up to her room early. The beautiful day was shading into a lovely evening, the sky streaked with crimson and gold that pierced the smoke. By now Maudelyn would be under a clearer sky, perhaps tossed on the sea that divided

England from the island where savage warriors played on harps. She winged her thoughts to him and then shook her head impatiently at her own foolishness. Two meetings and she could not get the lad out of her mind! The thought came to her that perhaps Petrella had felt like that about the young Godwin de Faucon and he had taken advantage of it.

Morning brought with it no easing of her dilemma. Her mother, glancing at her anxiously, said, 'You are well? I thought you very quiet when you came in yesterday.'

'I walked too far,' Diana said briefly.

'And you are apprehensive about the marriage.' It was a statement, not a question. 'You must not be too fearful, love. Remember that in matrimony women find their greatest happiness, and Godwin is a lusty man.'

'An experienced man?' Diana ventured.

'Would you have him a green lad at his time of life?' Kate demanded. 'His past is no concern of yours.'

'And mine? Would mine be any concern of his?'

'You with a past? Silly child!' Her mother gave her an indulgent smile.

'But there are things in my past,' Diana thought. 'There are two people to whom I cling and a ring of men closing in on me

137

and the name 'Becky', called over and over. And there is Alice, little Alice who died of the smallpox and whom my parents never mention.'

Aloud, she said, 'Do you know anyone called Becky?'

'Becky?' Kate considered then shook her head. 'No, I don't think I've ever met anyone of that name. Why?'

'No matter. Are you coming with me to the Todmores?'

'I think I will. I had meant to stay here and help Jane with the plucking of the chickens for tomorrow's meal, for the girl is sadly slow, but I think she may be trusted with them. Do you want us to go now, or is it too early? Mistress Todmore will not thank us for interrupting her in the middle of her work.'

'We can send Jane ahead before she starts on the chickens.'

'That's a sensible notion. I'll hurry her — oh, no, not a visitor! I wonder who is calling on us. Not Sir Godwin yet, for he is not due until this afternoon.'

'Shall I open the door and find out?' Diana said, as the knocking continued.

'Yes, indeed. Is my cap straight?' Kate worried.

'Very neat,' Diana assured her going to the door.

Peter Todmore, his pleasant face drawn, stood on the threshold, hurrying into speech with only the barest greeting.

'Mistress, good-day! I beg pardon but something very shocking has occurred. So very shocking that I thought it best to acquaint you with it myself, for I must go at once to Oxford.'

'What has happened?' Kate asked, drawing him within. 'Shall I fetch William? He is upstairs writing to the steward who is looking after the farm for us, but he will be down directly if I call.'

'I've time only to stop one moment,' he said. 'Good-morrow, Mistress Maundy. You'll pardon my haste?'

'When you tell us the reason for it,' Kate said.

'We just now received word,' he said. 'Master Ralph Aston, the father of my betrothed, is dead. I have come from identifying the body and must ride at once to Oxford. His family is staying there, and it's best that a friend should take the news.'

'Master Aston dead! But Diana went to Cheapside yesterday and nobody was at home,' Kate said.

'He was not found at home,' Peter said. 'He was found in Chelsea.'

'Found?' Diana's voice was a thread.

'Aye, in a field just outside Chelsea Village. 'Twas not a natural death,' Peter said grimly. 'He had been stabbed, and carried some distance before he was left. It was only by chance that he was recognised so quickly. The man who found him had bought cloth from him about a month since. The mystery is what Master Aston was doing in Chelsea, for he had no friends there. The gentleman who discovered the body was on his way from Southwark.'

'This is a shocking thing,' Kate said. 'I never met Master Aston, but I hoped to have that pleasure. It was robbery, I suppose?'

'He was not in the habit of carrying a lot of money,' Peter said. 'I fear that Mistress Aston will be quite cast down. You'll excuse me but I have to leave now.'

'Yes, of course. Poor Mistress Aston,' Kate said vaguely.

She was torn between sympathy for a woman she had never met and the natural excitement of being on the fringe of a murder enquiry.

'Mistress Maundy. Mistress Diana.' He bowed and hurried out again.

'This is a dreadful affair,' Kate said. 'Diana, you look ill. I do think Master Todmore could have broken the news more gently. And to think you were in Cheapside only yesterday! It makes my blood run cold when I think of it, though he was killed in Chelsea, was he not? Stabbed! I had better run up and let your father know. It is not as if we were acquainted with the Astons, but we had fully intended to call upon them before the wedding. I suppose we ought to delay our visit to Mistress Todmore. Do tell Jane to get those chickens plucked!'

She bustled upstairs, eager to tell William the news.

Diana sat down on a stool by the table and gazed after her mother's retreating back. She felt cold and sick and her hands were shaking.

Ralph Aston was dead. Found stabbed in Chelsea where he had no acquaintances. And that wasn't so. He knew that Sir Godwin de Faucon was living in Chelsea, and he knew that because she had told him so. He must have gone to face his old enemy.

'I swore I would kill him if I ever laid eyes on him again,' he had said.

But it was Ralph Aston who had been killed. Self defence might have served as a plea, but Godwin had not wished to make his connection with the Astons known.

'And he does not know that I have heard the story,' Diana whispered into her cupped hands. 'Dear Lord! he does not know that

I have even met the Astons.'

The sickness was growing worse, scalding her throat. She hurried to the basin and leaned over, retching.

'I knew you were not well!' Kate exclaimed, pattering down the stairs again. 'Excitement and now this dreadful news! I think we should postpone our visit to Chelsea. I will have word sent to Sir Godwin, and you must lie down whilst I make you a tisane. Your father is very greatly disturbed. Violence is something he detests!'

'And if I stop thinking,' the girl decided, 'Perhaps it will all be nothing but a dream, like the nightmare I've ridden on since I was a child.'

But she knew that both dreams sprang from reality, and the knowledge was a stone in her heart.

8

Sir Godwin came later that day. Diana, called down by her mother, had time in which to compose herself, but she was unusually pale.

' 'Tis the news of Master Aston's death,' Kate explained. 'Indeed we are all greatly upset by it, but Diana knew the family. Why, she went over to see them yesterday to invite them to the wedding, but nobody was at home.'

'I was sorry to hear about it,' Sir Godwin said. 'It is becoming more and more dangerous even to walk the streets.'

His tone was regretful, his face expressing no more than polite interest. Diana stared at him, unable to believe that he could be so bland when he must be guilty of the murder. Not murder! Self defence. It had to be self defence. Ralph Aston had attacked him and Sir Godwin had been forced to defend himself. It must have happened like that. There was no other explanation.

'You're very silent, mistress,' he commented.

'I am not well,' she evaded.

'You ought not to allow such a trivial

matter to discompose you,' he rebuked.

'Trivial? A man is dead!'

'Men die every day,' he said easily. 'They are killed in battle or fall victim to the plague. At least Master Aston died quickly.'

'How do you know that?' she frowned. They were in the garden and she paused in their walk to stare at him.

'I believe your father mentioned that he was stabbed in the back. I imagine he'd have died quickly.'

'Yes, I suppose so.' If that was true it meant that Master Aston was walking away when he was attacked.

'I wish you would put this wretched business out of your mind,' he complained. 'You have done nothing but talk about it since I came. It is all very tragic but we are to be wed very soon, and you ought to be talking about that.'

'I beg your pardon.' She tried to smile, but her eyes were still troubled and there was a decided spring in her step when Kate called her to come in to have a hot posset before Sir Godwin went back to Chelsea. It was a decided relief when he bade them goodnight, and she could not prevent a wry look when her mother said anxiously, 'Do have a care, sir! It is not safe to ride through the streets after sunset.'

'I will take great care, mistress,' Sir Godwin said, and for an instant Diana detected amusement at the back of his respectful gaze. It chilled her, as if she had seen corruption behind a mask.

That night she dreamed more vividly than before. Again she was very small, clinging to someone's hand, hearing the rushing of a river nearby and seeing, as the heavy clouds lifted and the moon shone briefly forth, the outlines of a building high on the hill opposite. Then the clouds rushed down again and she could see lights bobbing in the distance and the ring of grinning faces framed in unkempt hair, and hear her own voice calling over and over, 'Becky! Becky!'

Her voice was actual not a dream voice, and someone was shaking her upright. Kate, in wrapper and nightcap, her face puckered with concern, bent over her.

'Child! What in the world ails you? You shout loud enough to wake the dead!'

'Did I disturb father?'

'Lord, no! Nothing wakes William once his head's on the pillow,' Kate assured her, 'but I was restive myself. What ails you? Are you troubled about Master Aston's death?'

'That, and other matters.' Diana sat up, pushing the heavy hair out of her eyes.

'What matters?'

'Mother, who was Alice?' Diana blurted.

'Alice?' The familiar shutter came down.

'Alice Maundy who died of the smallpox. Who was she?'

Kate's round face was greenish in the candlelight, but Diana pressed on.

'Who was she, my lady mother? I saw you in the chapel, mourning for her. Was she my sister, and if so, why don't you speak of her? And who am I ? I have dreams of a place I've never seen and I grieve for someone I never knew. Why? What secret is there that Dame Marjorie knows and that you and my father conceal?'

'So it has to be out.' Her mother spoke at last, her voice infinitely sad. 'All these years and now it has to be out. I have been expecting this since we came back from London.'

'Who was Alice?' Diana asked.

Kate sat down on the edge of the bed and looked at her hands as if the answer were there.

'Alice was my daughter,' she said at last. 'She was my little girl. I had miscarried five times before she was born and we feared I would never bear a living child, for I was near forty and my flowers were drying up. Then Alice was born. She would be my last child, the physician said, and we cherished her more on that account. She was such a sweet, merry child. We came to London with her, and took lodgings here for three months. It was a holiday, the first William and I had ever had. We hoped that Alice would enjoy it, and she did. She loved the market place and the lions at the Tower, and people noticed her, you know, because she was such a pretty, friendly child.'

'What happened?' Diana asked.

'She fell sick,' Kate said. 'She fell sick and the fever grew higher and higher, and then she died. She just died, in a few hours. Smallpox, the physician said, and he condoled with us. We wanted to take her home with us, but there was difficulty in travelling because the peasants rose up and marched on London. So we laid her here and waited until it was safe to leave again.'

'But who am I?' Diana whispered.

'We found you,' Kate said. 'I went to the chapel to pray for Alice. It was the last day of our visit here, for the rebellion was crushed and Wat Tyler dead.'

'Yes?' Diana whispered the word for Kate's expression was remote as if she was living in that other period of her life.

'I knelt and prayed,' Kate said, 'or perhaps it wasn't a prayer. More a kind of questioning over and over, why it had happened when we loved her so much. And then I looked up and saw you crouching in a corner of the chapel, crouching there with your hair all over your face and staring at me. You must have wandered in, I suppose, and hidden there. It seemed you'd been sent to me, and when I held out my hand you took it and came back to the lodgings with me.'

'But didn't you try to discover where I'd come from?' Diana exclaimed.

'There was little use in trying,' Kate said. 'The city was crammed with people for many had sought refuge within the walls from the peasant army. William made some enquiries but nobody came foward to claim you. And you would say nothing except the name 'Diana'. Over and over, pointing to yourself and saying 'Diana'. The physician said you had had a shock of some kind and could not remember. You were well-nourished and your garments were of good quality though they were torn and stained.'

'The seal,' Diana interrupted. 'Who gave me the seal?'

' 'Twas clenched tight in your hand and you'd not give it up,' Kate said. 'So we left it with you. And we took you home with us, back to Devon.'

'You stole me?'

'Nobody claimed you,' Kate said obstinately, 'and you would say nothing to us except 'Diana'. We could not have left you to starve or be mistreated. You became our new daughter, and it has seemed like that ever since, as if you had been born to us. At the farm you grew up happily, beginning to talk and laugh. The neighbours were understanding. They agreed that it was kinder to have you grow up to believe you had always been ours, and you did, didn't you? You have been our dear daughter.'

'Dame Marjorie began to tell me.'

'The poor soul is a little crazed and means no harm,' Kate said. 'We brought you to London in hopes of finding a husband for you. I was a little uneasy but nobody remembered you.'

'Does Sir Godwin know this?' Diana asked.

It was odd but the news had not much shocked her, as if deep down she had known it all the time.

'Gentlemen are not much disposed to marry foundlings, even when they are pretty and have good dowries,' her mother said.

'And I am not much disposed to marry Sir Godwin,' Diana flashed.

'You are not still dreaming of the young man who went to Ireland? I warned you that some dreams are not meant to come true.'

'It's nothing to do with that,' Diana interrupted, 'I went to the Astons' house in Cheapside — '

'And found them from home. You told us.'

'Master Ralph Aston was at home,' Diana said. 'He invited me in and I told him about my betrothal. And he said that he knew of Godwin de Faucon.'

'Knew him? Are you sure?'

'He knew him well, for they grew up together,' Diana said. 'Their paths separated, for Godwin went to Flanders and Ralph Aston became a merchant in Cheapside. He was betrothed to a neighbour's daughter and then Godwin came back, and seduced her, and left her with child. She miscarried of the babe and died, but Godwin had gone abroad again. Master Aston married another lady, but he never forgot what Godwin de Faucon had done, and he never forgave.'

Her mother was looking at her with an appalled expression.

'Master Aston was — killed last night,' she breathed at last.

'He made me tell where Sir Godwin was lodging,' Diana confessed. 'I think he went to see him, to warn him not to marry me, I think Sir Godwin killed him, stabbed him in the back as he was leaving.'

'We have no proof.' Kate twisted her hands together.

'It's a rare chance that has a man killed by strangers when he is walking away from his enemy,' Diana said. 'Would you leave me to wed such a man?'

'The papers are signed and the licence bought,' Kate said helplessly. 'If he wishes to marry you he can take you to Court for breach of promise and ruin us all.'

'Not if I tell the reason for breaking the marriage contract.'

'My love, you must do no such thing!' Kate said. 'If you're right, then you would stand in grave danger if Sir Godwin ever discovered what you suspected. Murder is a hanging matter!'

'But I cannot wed him,' Diana said. 'Cannot you tell him that I am a foundling? You said yourself that a gentleman didn't want to marry girls of unknown parentage. Sir Godwin is a proud man who has served at Court. He won't have any wife who doesn't know her beginnings.'

'Your father would be very angry. He always swore that we would never tell you, never tell anybody about you.'

'Because deep down he is ashamed of my beginnings.'

'No, he loves you so much that he cannot bear to remember you were not born to us,' Kate said quickly. 'He could not endure it, my dear. You must never tell him what you have discovered. For my sake, you must never tell him!'

'Then I am to be married to Sir Godwin?' Diana whispered. 'Is that what you want for me? He is a man without scruples or honour, and I don't love him or have any affection for him. You can't want such a life for me!'

But Kate was not really listening. Instead she was rearranging her face into its usual placid smile, trying to make them both believe that the situation was not as bad as it appeared.

'Young men are often foolish and hot blooded, and 'tis probable the wench led him on. Master Aston obviously nursed a grudge for many years, and that is an unchristian thing to do. Certainly we cannot judge a man by actions committed long ago.'

'The murder was last night,' Diana pointed out.

'And there is no proof,' Kate said. 'Perhaps Master Aston changed his mind and turned back when he was on his way to Chelsea, and thieves set upon him.'

'He would have been on horseback.'

'He might have taken a boat,' her mother

said. 'I think it very likely that he did take a boat. Then he would have been on foot and the robbers could have crept up behind, plunging their daggers into him.'

'Or Sir Godwin could have done so, inviting him in, promising not to see me again and then killing him as his suspicions slept!'

'Because of a youthful scandal he didn't wish you to know about? Then he must love you deeply to value your opinion so highly.'

'He wants to have his will,' Diana said, and shivered.

'You can prove nothing,' Kate repeated, 'and you can never ask him, nor break this contract without putting yourself in great danger lest your suspicions be true. Sir Godwin is a man in the prime of life, and I believe he does love you. Take comfort in that, for it means much to be loved.'

There was no help here. Diana gave her mother a despairing look and lay down again.

'You won't tell your father?' Kate said. 'We have thought of you as our own child for so long. He is so pleased with this marriage he has arranged for you.'

Her voice and eyes pleaded. And somewhere, thought Diana, is my own mother who lost me long ago. Doesn't she deserve something too?

'I think I can sleep now,' she said aloud.

'And you are not angry with me for what happened so long ago?'

'You have always been my lady mother,' Diana said steadily. 'Knowing I wasn't born to you doesn't alter that. I still feel the same.'

'I'll see you in the morning.' Kate bent to kiss her and went softly to the door, relief in every line of her plump body.

Alone, Diana stared into the dimness. So she was not, as she had been bred to believe, Diana Maundy at all. She was Diana Someone or other from a place she didn't know, and she was to be married to a man who was very likely a ruthless killer. A man must be ruthless to be prepared to kill for the sake of protecting the secret of something that had happened when he was young.

Lying there she knew that she could not go through with it. Regardless of the consequences she could not bear to vow love and obedience to a man whom she could neither love nor obey.

But there seemed no way in which she could avoid what was ahead of her. There was nobody to whom she could turn for help, nobody powerful enough to protect her from Sir Godwin de Faucon — except the Duke of Lancaster. At that thought Diana sat bolt upright in bed, her eyes wide.

'John of Gaunt,' she breathed. 'He spoke to me kindly, and he is Maudelyn's father. If I go to him then he will help me. I know he will.'

She felt her spirits lift almost as if she had already gained an audience with the duke and her problem was solved. Sighing as she lay down again, closing her eyes and beginning to make plans as she waited for the dawn to come.

At breakfast William announced his intention of going over to Cheapside.

'Although we have never met the Astons I do feel obliged to pay my respects if they are returned from Oxford,' he said a trifle fussily. 'You will accompany me. Won't you, Kate?'

'Yes, of course.' Kate darted a little anxious look at Diana who said at once,

'You need not fret about me, my lady mother. I shall stay here, if that pleases you.'

'The poor child has a headache,' Kate excused. 'With all the excitement of the wedding and poor Ralph Aston's death 'tis scarcely to be wondered at! It will do you

155

good to rest quietly here, while your father and I go to the Astons. Poor lady! a word of sympathy won't come amiss, I feel. Such a terrible thing to happen!'

'London is a dangerous city,' William agreed. 'You must not wander out again by yourself, Diana.'

She sat, outwardly quiet, as her parents bustled about. It was a fine morning but there was a nip in the air, and Kate was torn between a summery mantle and a warmer one lest the weather suddenly change. Then William decided it would be more sensible to delay their going until the afternoon to give the Astons more time in which to have returned from Oxford.

The morning dragged by on leaden feet. Diana, pleading headache, went and lay down on her bed, willing herself to be still and quiet, fearful lest rain clouds obscure the sky. If her parents decided to stay at home there was no way in which she could slip out.

The day remained fine and by midafternoon William and Kate (in the warm cloak) were ready.

'We won't be more than an hour or two,' Kate said, kissing her. 'We'll just introduce ourselves and leave our condolences. It's very likely that Mistress Aston won't be in a fit state to see anybody. I'm sure that I wouldn't be if anything happened to your father!'

'Tell Jane we'll be back in time for supper,' William instructed.

She nodded, smiling, willing them to hurry. Now that she had to seek an audience of the duke she wanted to carry out her intention before her resolution faltered.

They left at last, having turned back to assure her they didn't intend to linger in Cheapside but would return before dark, and she was to be sure to lock the door and not let anyone strange in.

Apart from Jane, who was in the kitchen weeping over shredded onions, Diana had the lodging to herself. She hurried upstairs as soon as she was certain that William and Kate had really gone and changed into the gown she had worn at the banquet, covering it with her travelling cloak. Thus attired she would be able to pass unnoticed in the streets but, with the cloak removed, her dress would proclaim her status as a gentlewoman and make it easier for her to gain admittance to the duke. At the last moment, for good fortune, she put the claw seal into her purse.

'Are you going out, mistress?' Jane, red-eyed and sneezing, emerged from the back quarters as Diana reached the foot of the staircase.

'Yes, I have some urgent business to attend,' Diana said.

'But your lady mother said we were to stay indoors,' the maidservant said.

'Do mind your own business and leave me to mine,' Diana said sharply.

'Yes, mistress,' Jane mumbled and vanished into the kitchen again.

Diana opened the front door and hesitated on the step. The wisest course of action would be to take a boat to the Savoy Palace, for that was the Duke's residence when he was in London. There was a landing stage no more than a couple of streets away where boatmen plied for hire. Closing the door behind her she went down the steps into the quiet street. It was hard to realise they were in the centre of the city but she had discovered that there were dells of privacy even in this bustling metropolis.

There was a boat waiting and its owner, a burly fellow with a good natured face, agreed to take her to the Savoy Palace for what seemed to be a reasonable sum.

He helped her into the rocking craft, assured her that he would make good time without endangering her, bit the coin she gave him with a practised air and applied himself to his task. Diana, her hood over her head, sat silently watching the buildings and towers slide past. It was cool and fresh on the river, but she was too tense to begin to enjoy the experience. Exactly what she would say to the duke would depend, she thought, on what the duke said to her. He might regard her as a silly, hysterical wench and send her home again, but she thought it more likely that he would find some way in which to help her.

'This is the Savoy, mistress.' The boatman was leaning on his oars and staring at her. 'This is the watergate, but the main entrance is further on. Do you want me to wait for you?'

'No. That won't be necessary.' She accepted his helping hand to stand up and step onto the wooden landing stage, and walked beneath the arch of the watergate onto the wide path that snaked around the outer walls. The palace seemed to be a jumble of gateways and arches and high towers. They dwarfed her as she walked on, and the sun striking fire from the river dazzled her.

Her father had told her that the duke's palace had been a symbol for the peasants of the greed and power of the ruling classes and so, when the rebellion had broken out, they had burned it down. But the duke had rebuilt it more lavishly than before, and now added insult to injury by publicly stating

159

that he preferred his Warwickshire home of Kenilworth.

The gates stood open and appeared to be unguarded. There were several people, members of the household and tradesmen she guessed, passing in and out. Diana fell in behind a small group of chattering ladies in high hennins and followed them across a cobbled space and from thence to an inner yard where more archways led into a bewilderment of stables, kitchens and rose arbours. Nobody took the slightest notice of her, and for a moment she stood in confusion, wondering what on earth to do. Then her chin raised, determination in her blue eyes, she approached a soldier who leaned against one of the pillars and said, her voice only faintly tremulous, 'Conduct me to the Duke of Lancaster's apartments, if you please.'

9

The man, instead of questioning her or ordering her to be about her business as she had feared, merely said.

'This way, mistress, if you'll follow me.' It was unbelievably easy, she thought, as they threaded their way between the groups of chattering people. The inner rooms of the Savoy were smaller than she had expected, connected by long passages and flights of stone steps, but the tapestry that glowed against the walls, the carved furniture, the gilded coats of arms were evidence of immense wealth. The Savoy was like a many faceted jewel and at its heart was power.

'These are the Duke's apartments, mistress.' The soldier indicated a door. 'He's not in residence but his secretary will see to you.'

'Not in residence? Is he still at Westminster then?'

'No, mistress. His Grace sailed for Gascony three days since.'

'But I have to see the duke in person!' Diana exclaimed. 'It's urgent, imperative that I see him.'

'You could try swimming,' her guide said. 'You'll not catch him else.'

'The duchess — '

'Is at Kenilworth, mistress. You'll do much better to leave a message with His Grace's secretary,' the man said.

'I see. Thank you.' She smiled wanly, sensing that he was growing a little impatient, and stepped into the room. It was an antechamber with two high chairs and a table on which small ornaments were arranged. The tapestries depicted a hunting scene and at one end of the apartment carved double doors blocked her view.

The soldier had gone and she settled herself to wait, feeling increasingly nervous as the minutes went by. The duke's absence explained the ease with which she had penetrated thus far. No doubt the palace was more strictly guarded when he was in residence. If only he hadn't gone to Gascony! She could think of no way in which to put her story to a secretary. He would have her locked up for a crazy wench or thrown out for trespass.

She rose and went over to the table, wondering if there was a bell she was supposed to ring to summon whoever she wanted to see, but the objects on the table were delicate, pretty geegaws. A miniature tankard big enough for a child had a silver tailed mouse climbing up its side was next to a nest of yellow ducklings made out of brilliant yellow clay. There was a bottle filled with polished stones that winked and twinkled where the light caught them and a number of carved seals of ivory and silver. Diana caught her breath sharply and leaned closer, staring at the silver claw with its curved talons. It was an exact replica of the seal she possessed.

'Were you looking for something?' a voice enquired. A tall girl, attired in vivid golden brown, with reddish hair loose about her shoulders, had come in and was watching her inquisitively.

'These are all very pretty,' Diana said.

'They belonged to my father's first wife,' the girl said. 'She was the Duchess Blanche, you know, but she died long since. She was a very lovely creature they say, and had excellent taste.'

'That seal.' Diana pointed to the claw.

'She had two or three cast for her in the same design. My half-brother, Maudelyn, has one, I believe.'

'Your half-brother?' Diana turned and looked at the girl with more interest.

'I am Joan Neville, the Duke's youngest child.'

'Oh, I see.' Diana's tone was blank and the girl laughed, wrinkling up her nose.

'I doubt it, for nobody can ever sort out my father's children,' she said. 'The Duchess Blanche gave him two daughters and a son. Pippa is wed to Joachim of Portugal and Bet was married to John Holland. Henry is widowed now and has six of his own. By his second Spanish bride my father had a daughter Catalina, but my own mother is Katherine Swynford.'

'Who was made duchess not long since.'

'And we Beaufort children made legitimate,' the girl nodded. 'My name is Neville now because I was wed to Ralph Neville on my fifteenth birthday. Maudelyn is my father's son by another lady, but I don't believe she sees my father these days.'

'Did Maudelyn go to Ireland?' Diana asked.

'I believe he did. We are all of us constantly moving from one place to the next,' Joan said, 'so its hard to keep track of us all. I am off to Raby myself in a day or two. Was it Maudelyn you wished to see?'

'I wished to see the duke,' Diana said.

'My father is in Gascony,' Joan said. 'Does he know you?'

'I am Diana Maundy. Perhaps Maudelyn mentioned me?' The other girl thought for a moment, then shook her head. 'Maudelyn knows so many women,' she said apologetically.

'Oh.' Diana's heart dropped into her shoes.

'But you said it was my father you wanted to see.'

'On the question of my marriage,' Diana said awkwardly. 'I am to be wed, you see, to a man who — there are things I suspect about him that I must tell to the duke. I met His Grace, once, you see, and he spoke to me kindly. I hoped he might help me.'

'To avoid your marriage? He'll not interfere in private matters,' Joan said.

'But he has great power!'

'In affairs of state, yes, but I cannot believe your marriage would be an affair of state,' the girl began, then paused as a voice sounded beyond the door.

'Lady Joan! Lady Joan, where in the world are you?'

' 'Tis my governess!' Joan Neville grimaced. 'Is it not ridiculous that a married woman should have a governess!'

'If you could tell me who might be able to help me,' Diana pleaded.

'If I were you I'd marry the man and not try to find out too much about him,' Joan advised, then raised her voice to call, 'I'm coming! Do be patient!'

'But — ' Diana's hand fell to her side in a little gesture of defeat. The girl had whisked out again, her heels tapping on the stone.

She turned once more to the table, stretching out her hand to examine the silver claw seal. It was a distinctive design. Joan had said the Duchess Blanche had had two or three of them. How had one come into the possession of a lost child hiding in a chapel? A falcon's claw. Bastard children usually took their mother's name. Maudelyn Falcon. Godwin de Faucon. There was a link, but she was not clever enough to fathom it out.

'What business have you in here?' The voice was sharply suspicious and Diana jumped nervously, letting the seal fall with a clatter. The man who stood behind her was evidently an official of some kind, and equally obviously he was ill-pleased to find her there.

'I was — looking at these things,' she said foolishly.

'Stealing more like! These were the property of the late duchess and not to be touched!'

'I wasn't stealing,' she said haughtily. 'I have business with the duke's secretary.'

'Who is too busy to be bothered with wenches,' the official snapped. 'You're not employed here?'

166

'No. No, I'm visiting. On business.' Although she had done nothing wrong the man's cold stare made her blush guiltily.

'Are you indeed?' The man gave her another hard stare, then said abruptly, 'We'll make enquiries. Nobody sees Master Secretary without an introduction. Come along!'

It would have been useless and undignified to struggle. Her cheeks burning, she allowed him to take her arm and hustle her into the passage. He walked fast, grumbling under his breath. A pompous man who believed the security of the palace rested on his shoulders, she thought and might have found it amusing at any other time.

'You may cool your heels in here until I've leisure to deal with you,' the man said, opening a narrow door and thrusting her within. As she struggled to keep her balance the door slammed and a bolt grated home in its socket.

She was in some kind of storeroom. There were bales of cloth on the floor and light slanted down from a narrow window high in the wall. Diana looked round in helpless exasperation. The thickness of the walls, the heavy door, made it impossible for her to shout with any hope of being heard. Biting back her impatience she sat down on one of the bales of cloth and waited.

The light grew weaker and the sun sank. She was cold despite her cloak and aware of a rumbling in her stomach that reminded her that she had had no supper. After a while however her lids began to droop and she leaned back on the soft cloth and slept fitfully. She woke once with the moon shining in on her, and then slept again and dreamed, not of the ring of grinning savage faces but of a tall abbot walking with bound hands into a furnace that glowed white hot but did not burn.

She woke to cold, grey dawn and the sound of the bolt being drawn back. A servant stood in the doorway looking at her in surprise.

'I was locked in by mistake,' Diana said, jerking upright on the bales.

'All night? What a shame!' The man put out his hand to help her to her feet. 'Were you wanting something, mistress?'

'I came in by the water-gate,' Diana said. 'I was hoping to see the duke's secretary.'

'You'll not see any of the secretaries today,' the servant told her. 'My Lady Joan is preparing to return to Raby, and the duke's retinue are to escort her. Was it important?'

'No,' she said, disappointment flattening

her voice. 'No, it's not very important. Could you show me the way back to the water-gate?'

'This way, mistress.' He held the door open obligingly and she followed, pulling her hood well over her head as she went, lest the man who had accused her of stealing might see her. Probably he'd locked her up to give her a fright, and then forgotten about her, but she was nervous at the prospect of meeting him again.

It was as easy to leave the palace as it had been to enter it. She thanked the servant and walked out onto the river bank. This morning the river was grey and sullen, the clouds lowering, and there was a decided nip in the air. Diana shivered, glancing about her for a boat. She had failed in her attempt to seek help and by now her parents would be frantic with anxiety. It seemed that she was destined to marry Godwin de Faucon anyway, and to keep silent about her suspicions.

She had walked to the next landing-stage before a boat hove into view. The boatman was of the same surly mien as the weather, charging her more than the usual fare and grumbling that it was scarce worth his while to take only one passenger such a distance.

She scrambled out of the vessel as best she could. She was extremely hungry by now and her sleep had left her unrefreshed. The few people hurrying past glanced at her without much interest.

She stopped at a corner stall to buy a mutton pie and a jug of buttermilk. She was so late already that another half-hour would make no difference. There was also the possibility that her father might have one of his rare fits of temper and lock her up on bread and water to teach her better manners. So she might as well get some food inside her.

The pie was crusty and hot, the meat filling juicy and tasty. She chewed appreciatively, enjoying it consciously and putting the confrontation with her parents to the back of her mind.

The woman who had sold her the pie leaned her elbows on the stall and smiled, gap-toothed.

'You're my first customer this morning, mistress,' she said. 'Usually there's quite a crowd, but you're the first one today.'

'Perhaps it's early,' Diana suggested, swallowing the last of the pie.

'Nay, it'll be the murders.' The woman passed over a cloth for the girl to wipe her mouth and hands. 'I'd have gone round myself, but I'd my oven to attend.'

'Murders?' Diana, having drained the last

of the buttermilk, wiped the grease from her lips and hands.

'Not three streets away,' the woman said. 'Terrible it was, the screams and shouting. The maidservant got away over the garden wall and ran to the Todmores for help. Pleasant folk the Todmores. Their boy is a lawyer, you know, and doing very well.'

'Who was — where did it happen?' Diana asked. Her mouth had gone dry and her heart had begun to beat uncomfortably fast.

'Why, two visitors, mistress. That's the dreadful part of it, that they should be on holiday. Very respectable people who had taken the Drury house while their daughter's betrothal was being arranged.

The woman had begun to sway backwards and forwards and there was a mist descending. Diana found herself crouched on a stool, a hand at the back of her neck pressing down her head.

'Poor wench! You look fit to drop!' the woman exclaimed. 'Did you know the people then?'

'I think — they may have been friends of my own family,' Diana said dizzily. 'Do you know what happened?'

'Only what Jack Carpenter had to tell me. He's ostler at the stables and he was tending one of the mares when he heard the shouting.

171

He thought 'twas some tavern brawl and took no notice at the time, but then a man came riding past as if the devils of hell were at his heels!'

'What sort of man?'

'Big, fair-haired, with a red and furious face. Jack saw a glimpse of it by the light of the street torch, and then the man was gone. It's his belief he saw the killer. Mind, he didn't know there'd been a killing then, but he guessed something was afoot, so he left the horse and went to see, and ran straight into the Todmore's apprentice who had just roused the household when the maid climbed over the wall.'

'What — what did she say?'

'She was half out of her mind, poor soul!' The stallkeeper, despite her sympathy was obviously beginning to relish the telling of her tale. 'It seems her master and mistress had come in from a visit to a friend of theirs and their daughter was not at home. The maid had heard an argument and then her mistress had said something about not wanting her daughter to be matched with a murderer, and then there was a scuffle in the sitting room and a clatter. She looked in from the kitchen and saw her mistress lying with her head on the hearth and blood coming from her nose and ears, and her master struggling with the friend. She saw him fall and then she ran through the back into the garden and over the wall. Jack Carpenter said they were both dead and the man gone by the time the neighbours arrived. 'Tis a dreadful tale! And you say your family knows them?'

'I believe so.' The girl spoke automatically, her eyes wide and strained. 'What a dreadful thing to happen. Do you think the man will be caught?'

'More likely he'll go into Sanctuary,' the woman said. 'Or buy his way out of it if he's any gold. But 'tis a fearsome thing! Are you still feeling bad, mistress?'

'No, no. It was only the shock.' Diana rose, surprised to find that her legs were quite steady and her head clear. It was almost as if what had happened had numbed her senses. 'I ought to be on my way now. You've been very kind.'

'You go straight home, mistress,' the woman advised. 'I tell you this city is becoming more lawless every day. There are those who speak out against the Court, but in my opinion the nobility do keep order.'

'Thank you again.' She couldn't bear to stay and listen to the woman's ramblings for another moment.

'You're certain you're all right?' The stallholder looked at her curiously.

'Perfectly. Thank you.'

Diana began to walk away rapidly. She ought to go home, she supposed, to be told what had occurred, to have the Todmores take care of her. But there was still Godwin de Faucon. He was at large somewhere in the city and she had not the slightest doubt that he was looking for her. She was a danger to him with her knowledge of the Aston murder.

A few large spots of rain plopped down. Perhaps it would be wise to go to Cheapside to the Astons. Mistress Aston would surely help to conceal her.

'Be you Mistress Maundy?' A man had stepped out of the alley just ahead, barring her path.

'No,' she said sharply. 'No, I'm not!'

'You look like the wench I'm to watch for,' the man said. 'The gentleman described you.'

'You're mistaken,' she said breathlessly.

'He said you might be coming this way,' the man persisted. 'He said you'd likely go flying off to Cheapside.'

'He? Who is he?'

'A tall, fair gentleman,' the man said, 'with gold in his pockets and a manner of speaking that shows he means to be obeyed. Not a good man to cross, mistress.'

She could imagine that only too well and a shiver ran through her, but she controlled it, speaking with as much conviction as she could muster.

'Well, as I am not Mistress Maundy it doesn't interest me, so kindly let me pass!'

'You may come and tell him so yourself then,' the man grinned. 'He'd not be in a very good humour if I was to let you slip through my fingers.'

'I can give you gold.' She pulled out her purse, holding it before him as she backed away. 'I can give you gold if you'll let me pass.'

The man's eyes gleamed and he lunged forward, snatching the purse with long, bony fingers. She ducked beneath his arm and ran then, hearing his hoarse cries as she plunged into the labyrinth of narrow streets. The rain was falling faster now and her feet skidded on the cobbles.

She must have come round in a circle, for the open gates ahead were familiar. She ran through them and up the narrow path, flagged between the tombstones into the gloom of the chapel. At this hour it was empty, lit only by the faint glow of the candles.

Diana ran up the side aisle towards the Lady Altar, and flung herself down, sobs of fear and grief tearing through her. Her parents were dead, killed by Godwin de Faucon in a fit of murderous rage and now he was looking for her. She had no doubt that he would kill her too, so that she could never tell what she knew about the Aston murder.

Jane had seen what happened, but Jane was an ignorant servant girl who would be terrified out of her few wits if the authorities questioned her. Jane was no real threat to him.

There were probably other men looking for her, men with coarse faces and clutching hands whom Godwin de Faucon would pay for information. She rubbed her face with the corner of her damp cloak and tried to think clearly.

A figure was walking down the aisle towards her. She held her breath, willing herself into invisibility, but the man — it was a priest — came on steadily and paused to frown at her.

'What are you doing here?' he demanded.

'I am claiming Sanctuary,' she said quaveringly.

'Sanctuary! You scarce look old enough to have committed any crime unless it be a sin of the flesh.'

Her cloak had parted and he was staring

disapprovingly at her low necked brilliant blue gown. No doubt he mistook her for a penitent whore hiding from her bully.

'I need a place of refuge,' she said. 'Can you help me to one, father?'

'This is a chantry,' he said, still disapproving.

'But you could take me to some place?' she begged. 'You must know of convents, of houses where women may live secure from molestation.'

'Such a place costs money,' he said.

'I have a ring,' she tugged the emerald betrothal ring from her finger and held it out to him. 'It was given to me by a man I once knew. Oh, please, father, isn't it sufficient to buy me sanctuary?'

If she were turned away, she thought frantically, her last hope was gone.

'Do you have a name, child?' the priest asked abruptly.

'I am called Diana.'

'And your parentage?'

'I never knew them,' she said, and wept inwardly at this final betrayal.

The priest took the ring and spoke to her again. 'Come with me,' he ordered.

It was a renewal of hope and she followed him willingly.

Interlude

1400

The small, fair haired woman held the silver claw seal in her hand and gazed at it for a long time. She had been doing this for months ever since the pedlar had come to Marie Regina and she had seen it among the things he offered for sale. It was as if constant gazing would induce it to offer up its secrets. Long ago, as a girl, she had chosen it for herself at the invitation of the Duchess Blanche, and now it had come back to her. Too many people had handled it and it had lost both her own and Diana's vibrations. Yet she was certain the girl was still alive. It made no sense for her to find it again after so many years if Diana was dead. She clung to that.

The tower room in which she sat looked out over acres of meadow and woodland towards the rushing river at the other side of which the monastery crowned the tor. She had known that monastery since childhood, had learned her lessons in the Abbot's parlour, helped in the infirmary and the scriptorium where the manuscripts were copied and illuminated. She could remember the tall Abbot with his proud eyes and dignified manner, and remember too, how other monks had come and of how, much later, she learned he had been burned for devil worship. Yet he had been a good man and the men who had burned him had been good men too. That was the great tragedy that good men should destroy one another. It had happened with the king and his Bolingbroke cousin. There were those, who said Richard had been a cruel despot lavishing gifts upon his royal favourites, but she had always thought of him as the beautiful boy riding bravely into the midst of the rebellious peasants and so turning the tide of anarchy.

And she could not picture Henry of Lancaster as the usurper. To her he would always be the sturdy, red-haired child with whom she had fished for tiddlers in the stream at Kenilworth. Now he had made himself king and nobody was sure if Richard was alive or dead. Gida was glad that the duke had not lived to see the son he adored strike down the nephew to whom he had been devoted.

Tears rushed into Gida's eyes, for John of Gaunt had been the only man she had ever loved. she could see him still as he had been in youth, tall among his brothers, with his

179

red-gold hair flowing over the ermine collar of his cloak. All those years of silent loving had brought her one night of pleasure and then her son.

It was months since she had heard from Maudelyn. He was near thirty now, and in her view it was time he settled down and gave her some grandchildren, but Maudelyn didn't like to be tied down. He had spent years in Ireland and on his last brief visit to Marie Regina had told her he'd been offered a position at his half-brother's Court. That would mean more travelling up and down the countryside she supposed, and he had laughed, green eyes slanting, and told her that he'd been born with wings on his heels.

That too was strange because her favourite archangel had always been Raphael, who carried the caduceus of knowledge and wisdom, and the scales that were like those on which her mother had measured out the powdered herbs she used for her healing potions. Raphael had tiny wings on his heels.

Yet it was Diana who had flown, snatched up on that night of terror which Gida would remember for as long as she lived. She had never talked to Maudelyn about that night, never mentioned Diana. It was very doubtful if he remembered her, for Diana had been only a babe when she had given him into the care of his natural father, the duke.

Now, gazing at the seal, she felt as if some finger from the past had lit a candle of hope. The pedlar had bought it in Cheapside. It was the vaguest of clues, but she would make a start there. She would travel to London to see the Astons. There was bad blood between the Falcons and Astons, but it was possible that Ralph's bitterness had softened over the years. She would visit them, she decided, and pay her respects at old Dorothy's grave, and perhaps somewhere in that crowded quarter of the city was the clue that would lead her to Diana.

She would start as soon as the weather was fine, she decided, and not return until her task was completed.

Part Two

10

1403

It had rained heavily for more than a week, overflowing the gutters and filling the crevices between the cobbles. The messenger wrung water out of his cloak and cursed under his breath. He was accustomed to travelling in inclement weather, but this was June, and in June one expected a little sunshine. It had been a fine, green spring with every promise of a warm summer, but now the rain was threatening to wipe out the crops and ruin the harvest. It had also made travelling more difficult, wetting one through to the skin and making it impossible to ride more than a few miles a day.

The outer walls of the convent displayed themselves briefly through the curtain of rain. The messenger rode up to the barred gate and reached for the bell rope. As he tugged it the bell clanged loudly within, startling his horse. There was a long pause, then an aperture appeared in the wooden panels and an eye stared up at him unblinkingly.

'Richard Descant, herald to His Grace King Henry the Fourth, requests an interview with the Prioress.'

He made his announcement in a loud voice and waited. Experience had taught him it was useless to be impatient when dealing with the religious, but he hoped that the extern sister would see fit to admit him before he was fairly drowned in the downpour.

The eye withdrew, the wooden panel was slid into place, and the gate creaked wide. He rode into the yard and dismounted, blinking through rain encrusted eyelashes at the stout nun who was barring the gates again.

'The stable is on your left, master,' she said. 'When you've seen to your horse come into the kitchen.'

He thanked her, and went into the warm, dry stable. Half an hour later, his cloak steaming by the fire, he sat at a table with a meal of pork stew and dumplings before him and reflected that one advantage of a wet journey lay in the comfort of its ending.

'So you come from the king's Court?' The extern sister was quite prepared to gossip.

'Yes, sister. I am herald to His Grace.'

'And ridden from Westminster? 'Tis foul weather!'

'Good for ducks,' he said.

'And you have business with the Prioress? Not bad news, I hope?'

'Nothing bad,' he assured her.

'We live so retired here,' she said, 'that sometimes news doesn't reach us for months, and often its bad news. Very bad news, sometimes, as when poor King Richard was murdered.'

It would not have been wise to say such a thing at Court where word had been put about that Richard had starved himself to death out of pique because he had been deposed.

'When you're ready, the Prioress will see you,' the nun said. 'We make no provision for visitors, but you may bed down with your horse and I'll make you some breakfast before you leave.'

'I thank you.' He soaked his bread in the dregs of the stew, and stood up. The extern sister led him out of the kitchen, across a covered yard, and down a narrow corridor into the parlour. Behind the barred grille, her face veiled against the gaze of a man, the Prioress sat with folded hands.

'Deo Gratia.' She made formal greeting, her hand signing a cross upon the air. 'Master Descant, you come from the king?'

'Yes, madam.' He snatched off his feathered cap and bowed.

'Sit down, Master Descant. His Grace is well, I trust?'

'But occupied with the rebellion in Wales.'

'Always unrest and trouble,' she said sadly. 'I am past fifty and have never known true peace, save in these convent walls. But we have heard that the king had wed.'

'To the Princess Joanna of Navarre,' he nodded. 'Indeed the message I bring comes from the queen rather than from the king.'

'Yes?' Her voice lifted with interest.

'Her Grace intends to appoint six new attendants,' he explained. 'Unmarried, young, and of good character. She wishes the opportunity to be given to those who are not of noble birth, though she does expect a certain standard of education.'

'And she hopes to find such a person here?'

' 'Tis well known that many young women of good character lodge in religious houses but do not actually take the vows.'

'But why this convent? We are not a rich or important House!'

'Her Grace wished to honour some of the lesser known convents,' he explained. 'This one is noted for its strict observance of the Rule.'

'That is true,' she admitted. 'His Lordship the Bishop congratulated me on the fact after his last visitation.'

'I believe that Her Grace acted upon the recommendation of the bishop,' he said.

'What duties would the post entail?' she asked.

'The usual ones of attendance upon the queen, who has agreed to be responsible for the young women and to provide dowries if any of them would care to marry.'

'And this young woman is to be escorted to Court?'

'To Westminster, madam.'

'There will be someone ready to go with you in the morning,' she said, after a brief pause for thought. 'Deo Gratia.' She rose and pulled down the heavy leather blind that hid her completely from view.

The messenger's retreating footsteps were muffled on the stone. A pleasant young man, she considered. She had had a lover once, before she had dedicated her life to God, and the young man had reminded her of him. For herself she had no regrets at all, because her life had satisfied her innermost nature, but she occasionally spared a thought for her lover, and hoped that he too had been content.

Such contentment was a blessing, and

she knew it was not bestowed upon all women who entered the cloister. Even some of those who requested permission to take their vows would, she surmised, be happier in the world.

After a long time she went into her own room. As Prioress she enjoyed the privilege of an apartment where she could sit alone. It was an austere chamber with only a small fire burning in the hearth, and a carved prie-dieu beneath a silver crucifix.

Cautiously, for her joints stiffened in wet weather, the Prioress knelt, folding her hands, composing herself for a prayer. A young woman of good character and some education might stand an excellent chance at Court of making her way in the world, even of snaring a husband if the queen provided a dowry. The problem lay in the choice of such a woman.

After a little while, for she was no believer in long prayers, she rose and rang the small bell on her table. Sixteen rings to summon the girl who had been brought to her eight years before and had not left the cloister since. 'Deo Gratia.' She raised her hand as Diana came in and knelt for her blessing.

'You wished to see me, Madam?' The girl had never addressed her by the more intimate 'Mother', used by the others. It was as if, in such small ways, she held herself apart from the rest of the community.

'Sit down, child.'

The Prioress pointed to a stool and, as Diana obeyed, leaned back in her own chair, studying her intently.

Diana would be in her mid-twenties, she guessed, but her years in the convent had preserved her look of youthful inexperience. The simple brown habit suited her fair colouring and her bearing was modest and quiet, but her blue eyes blazed with life and tendrils of yellow hair escaped from beneath her coif.

'Have you considered my request?' she asked now.

'To take the veil?' The Prioress frowned slightly, 'I have considered it most thoughtfully, child. Your request is not an unusual one, but I wonder if it springs from the heart. No, let me finish! I know you believe yourself to be sincere, but I am not happy in my own mind. Oh, you have worked hard since you came to us, and yet you are not one of us. We have our lives here within these walls but you seem to have left your real life beyond the walls. I see you look through the window sometimes into the garden and your foot taps as if you were impatient to be wild and free.'

'I've sacrificed all that,' Diana said swiftly.

'Sacrifice is of no value unless it is replaced by something more valuable,' the Prioress said. 'There is only one good reason for taking the veil, and that is for the sake of love. Nothing less will do. We cannot hide in a cloister because we fear or dislike the outside world. You know, I accepted you on trust but I am certain now that there is a human love waiting for you, and I cannot allow you to cheat yourself by denying that.'

'I had a dream once,' the girl said in a low voice. 'I was advised to forget it.'

'There are other dreams,' the Prioress said, 'and you are young and beautiful.'

'Must nuns be old and ugly?' Diana countered.

'By no means, but they do not usually whistle when they think that nobody is watching them,' the Prioress said with a gleam of humour. 'Neither do they curl their hair in the privacy of their cells.'

'I shall do penance,' Diana promised.

'There is no sin in greeting a blackbird or in making oneself comely,' the Prioress said. 'But there is very great sin in lying to oneself, child, and that is what you are doing when you declare you are ready to take the veil and deny every dream you ever had.'

'Then I am refused.' A mulish expression

settled on her features.'

'But that wasn't why I sent for you,' the Prioress said. 'There was a messenger came today, from the king's Court.'

The mulish look was chased away by one of fear. The Prioress noted it, and wondered, but went on calmly. 'He wished me to recommend a young woman suitable to act as an attendant to the new queen. She must be of good character, and it is probable that, should she wish to marry, the queen will provide her dower. I have decided to recommend you.'

'To go to Court? Oh, no, madam, it wouldn't do!' Diana's cheeks had flushed crimson and she was stammering slightly.

'Is something to your disadvantage known about you at Court?'

'No, why should it be?'

'Because I know nothing of you myself,' the older woman said patiently. 'The priest who brought you to us declared that in his opinion you were a repentant whore. I never believed so, for I flatter myself I can tell the difference between a harlot and a virgin — and I am certain you are a virgin. But I never questioned you, never asked you if you had any other name except Diana.'

'It is Maundy,' the girl said in a low voice. 'Diana Maundy. My — parents are dead, and I was to be married to a man I hated and feared. That's why I fled.'

'And do you seriously think that after so many years this man will be waiting to seize you as you ride through the convent gates?'

'I suppose not,' Diana muttered.

'And this dream you spoke about? It was another young man, of course.'

'He went away to Ireland,' Diana said. 'He is probably wed by now and has forgotten all about me.'

'And if he has not? My dear, isn't it possible that he still thinks of you?'

'If we're meant to meet again, then we will,' Diana said.

'But not within these walls.'

The Prioress spoke with decision. 'I have decided that you will ride to Westminster with Master Descant tomorrow morning.'

'So soon?' There was both apprehension and excitement in the pretty voice.

'The world waits for you,' said the Prioress. 'Deo Gratia.'

Emerging from the apartment into the chilly gloom of the unheated cloister Diana was tugged this way and that by conflicting emotions. In the years since she had seen him Godwin de Faucon had assumed gigantic proportions in her mind. In nightmares she ran down dark alleys and he was always waiting for her at the end of them, his dagger dripping red. But it was surely more probable that he had fled to another country and would not dare to return. And the Prioress was right when she said that Diana had asked to take the veil out of fear. She had lived with her fear for so long that it had become a habit as meaningless as the novice's habit she wore.

In her narrow cell with it's grey-blanketed pallet, its bowl and jug, three legged stool and plain, wooden cross, she stood for a few moments staring through the tiny barred window into the rain soaked garden.

Often she had stood thus, gazing out and trying not to remember the fields that had stretched around the farm. In the cloister day followed day with nothing to mark one from the other. Now she admitted to herself with reluctance that she had been extremely bored for much of her time here, and having admitted that she was filled with sudden excitement. To be attendant upon the queen was an opportunity for any young woman. She had never forgotten that banquet when she had been presented to King Richard and had spoken to John of Gaunt. Well, they were both dead now and Gaunt's son sat upon the throne. Times changed and life was waiting for her. Under the coarse cloth of the habit her flesh was firm and unblemished, her breasts high, her hips curving from a narrow waist. She was ripe for mating, she knew, and the knowledge warmed her.

'Diana, Mother Prioress tells me that you're leaving!' Sister Magdalen her eyes wide, was in the doorway.

'To be attendant to the new queen,' Diana nodded.

'Joanna of Navarre? They say her father was a madman. He died in the most terrible way, set alight accidentally by a candle when he was being treated for dropsy with cloths soaked in oil. He was burned alive, with none of his family near to help!'

'How do you know all that?' Diana asked.

'One hears rumours,' Sister Magdalen said vaguely. 'They say the new queen is very strange too. Perhaps she has inherited her father's madness.'

'That would be interesting anyway,' Diana said cheerfully.

'But to go to Court! Will you not be afraid of all the corruption there?' Sister Magdalen who would not have recognised corruption if she had been pushed into it head first, looked anxious.

'I shall avoid it, sister,' Diana said solemnly.

'Perhaps you will find a husband,' the

other breathed. 'They say the queen has promised to give a dowry.'

'Sister, you know about things quicker than anybody else in the convent!' Diana exclaimed, laughing.

'Because I have sharp ears,' Sister Magdalen said, returning her smile.

'I am going to miss you,' Diana said impulsively. 'I am going to miss you all!'

'For a little while, perhaps, but in a month or two you will begin to forget us,' Sister Magdalen said, and for a moment sadness pierced her tranquil face. 'When I came into the cloister my family all promised to visit me. They did, at first, but then my parents died and my brothers were wed, and now — why, it must be ten years since I had word of them.'

'I'll come back and visit you,' Diana promised. 'I'll ride a fine horse and wear a beautiful gown, and introduce you to my handsome husband. He will be very rich too, of course.'

'Of course,' Sister Magdalen agreed, and they laughed again until the little nun remembered that it was strictly forbidden for the sisters to enter one another's cells and trotted away to do some penance.

Yes, she would miss them but even as she thought that, she was beginning to wonder what style of dress the ladies were wearing at Court this season.

By morning the rain had eased off and a frail sun struggled weakly through the clouds. Diana, a heavy cloak over her gown, waited for the Prioress. The bag containing her shifts had been tied to the horse already, and the herald was waiting.

'He has hired a mount for you from the village, which is most resourceful of him,' Sister Magdalen had said.

'To ride a horse again,' Diana breathed.

'In a velvet riding skirt,' said Sister Magdalen and, in defiance of the Rule, put her arms about the younger woman and hugged her fiercely.

'Deo Gratia.' The Prioress had entered without her realising it, and she dropped hastily to her knees.

'My blessings on you, child,' the Prioress said. 'You are all ready, I see.'

'Yes, madam.'

'And happier about what has occurred? You are not still hoping to take your vows?'

'If you had agreed I would have sworn them and kept them,' Diana said.

'I know you would, child, and I want you to remember that if you change your mind and discover that your true life is here you are welcome to return.'

'There is one thing, madam.' Diana hesitated, then rushed on, 'You know my name now.'

'And will reveal it to nobody. When someone enters these walls she is dead to the world, and when she goes out into the world again she is dead to us. I wish you would trust me sufficiently to tell me the name of the man you fear so greatly.'

'He is called Godwin de Faucon,' she said reluctantly.

'De Faucon? No, the name isn't familiar to me,' the Prioress said. 'If I were you I would put him right out of my mind. Be a good wench, and remember us in your prayers.'

'Yes, I will. I promise you.' She knelt again briefly, her eyes lowered respectfully.

'The Lord keep you, child.' The shapely hand moved to sketch the cross over her head and the Prioress moved away.

The extern sister was unlocking the door. Diana took a deep breath and stepped out into the passage.

'Master Descant is mounted and waiting,' the sister said. 'You have breakfasted?'

'Yes, sister,'

'Here are some gingerbread men. I made them this morning. You eat them along the way now.'

'Yes, sister.'

'And don't get into any mischief at Court.' The extern nun who regarded all her enclosed sisters as wayward children spoke severely.

'No, sister.' Diana spoke meekly, the corners of her full lips twitching.

'Then get along, and God keep you, child.' Diana bowed and went into the yard. The gate was open and the cobbles gleamed wet on the road beyond. For a moment she shivered. Then a pleasant faced young man swung himself from his own horse and came to help her mount, startled admiration in his eyes as he glimpsed her face. She was lifted to the saddle where she clung, nervous for an instant. Then a surge of excitement rippled through her and she lifted her head and smiled.

'We will be there by suppertime,' the herald said.

'At Westminster?' She had almost said that she had been there already.

'It's a very large place, but Her Grace has her own apartments there and her attendants have their own dormitory too,' he said as if to reassure her.

'Have you met the queen?'

'Oh, yes, mistress. She's a fine lady,' he said.

'I shall look forward to serving her,' Diana

said, and wondered if Sister Magdalen had been wrong in her information. Perhaps Joanna of Navarre was not strange at all.

After a little while, when she was more accustomed to the motion and the unexpected view of fields and woods after the blinkered viewpoint of the narrow cloister, she ventured to ask.

'Does the name De Faucon mean anything to you, sir?'

'De Faucon?' He considered for a moment and then shook his head. 'I don't know everybody at Court of course, but the name is not familiar to me. Was it important?'

'No,' she said, her heart lifting. 'No, it wasn't important at all.'

All that mattered was that, after eight years, she was riding to Court and the sunshine was growing stronger. It was a day for new beginnings, a day for dreaming again.

11

Gida had not felt her years until this moment when she stood in the rain in front of the Aston house. It was so much smaller and shabbier than she remembered, and when she stepped within the eagerness with which the assistant hurried to greet her hinted that trade was bad.

'I was looking for Master Aston,' she said pleasantly. 'Master Ralph Aston?'

'My father died some years ago,' the young man said. 'I am Giles Aston.'

'Ralph is dead? Oh, but I am sorry to hear that,' she said, distressed.

'Were you a friend of my father's?' he enquired politely.

'At one time, long ago, we were brought up together,' she explained. 'My name is Gida Falcon.'

'My father occasionally mentioned you,' Giles said. 'Your fathers were friendly, I believe.'

'And when Ralph's parents and my own mother died, Dorothy cared for us, until at fourteen I was sent to Court and Dorothy brought Ralph here. I stayed here myself for a considerable time at one period but our paths separated after that and we lost touch. Your mother — is she?'

'My mother died two years since.'

'I never met her,' Gida said. 'It seems I've come on a fools errand then.'

'But you must certainly stay for a while,' Giles said quickly. 'I'll see to the stabling of your horse and then you must come upstairs and take some refreshment. My sister and her husband are coming for the evening. I'll close the shop. It's not likely anyone will call.'

'This was a prosperous little business,' Gida remarked, unable to keep the note of criticism out of her voice.

'I had ambitions for it,' Giles said ruefully. 'I believed I could find a method of dyeing the cloth in brilliant shades that held fast in water. I fear my method has proved costly, for I had to raise my prices to meet my increased expenses and so people cease to buy.

'I am left with bales I cannot sell, and debts to be paid before I dare to lower my prices again.'

'I'm sorry for it,' she said gently, thinking that he was too young to look so careworn.

'I'll see to your horse.' He hurried out, leaving her to look round the dim shop with its bales of gaudy wool and its flat counter.

She had come here to bear the child conceived in that one night of pleasure with the duke, and she had left secretly and in haste.

'Shall we go upstairs, mistress?' The young man had returned and was shepherding her up the narrow stairs.

'We'll eat when Enid and Peter arrive,' he said.

'Your sister?'

'She is wed to a lawyer,' he explained, 'and they live over near Temple Bar, but they visit me every week.'

'I shall be happy to meet them.'

'But you came to see my father. I ought to have written to let you know about him, but it was such a terrible time, with my mother too shocked to attend to anything, and myself no more than a lad.'

'What happened?' She gave him her cloak and sat down.

'He was killed — stabbed,' Giles said. 'My mother and Enid and I were in Oxford attending a wedding at the time, and the news was brought to us. He was found in Chelsea though we had no acquaintances there. It was perhaps a whim on his part to go out there but we will never know.'

'That's dreadful.' She spoke automatically, because it had been so many years since she had seen him that he had grown shadowy in her mind.

'My mother never really recovered from it,' Giles said sombrely. 'I believe that she was glad to die. But tell me about yourself, mistress. Have you come far?'

'From Kent,' she said briefly.

'Unescorted? You ran a great risk.'

'At my age the risk is very small,' she said dryly. 'To be frank with you I have been putting off this journey for three years.'

'Oh! Why?' He sat down opposite her.

'Out of fear,' she said slowly. 'It was not simply to visit your father that I came. I have another task to perform, and have delayed its beginning because I felt, I suppose, that the end might be a sad one.'

'I don't understand you, mistress,' he said.

'Have you ever seen this before?' She held out the claw, watching his face anxiously as he examined it.

'No, mistress. I've not seen one like that before,' he said at last.

'A pedlar sold it to me and said it came from Cheapside. This seemed the logical place to begin.'

'To begin what?' he asked.

'The seal belonged to a girl I knew,' she said. 'I lost trace of her many years ago, and then by chance this came into my hands again.'

'Three years ago?' he said surprised. 'Mistress, why did you wait so long?'

'I told you, because I feared to find out there was really no hope.'

'Was she your child?,' he asked.

This was the question she had dreaded, but Ralph's death made it easier. To his son she need tell only part of the truth.

'When I was staying here in Cheapside,' she said slowly, 'there was a girl, a neighbour's daughter. The name Petrella — have you heard it?'

He shook his head.

'Well she was a sweet girl but a man, a knight just back from France, took advantage of her innocence and when he found she was with child deserted her. Nobody would have anything to do with her, even her parents threatened to lock her up in a convent. I was due to return into Kent anyway, so I left in haste and took Petrella with me. She died there in giving birth to a child, a daughter.'

'The girl you seek?'

'She was just four years old,' Gida said, and her eyes were clouded with remembered pain. 'We knew there was a rebellion afoot. The peasants were banding together against the masters, and respectable folk were in fear of their lives and properties.'

'Yes, mistress?' He was leaning forward intently.

'I feared the castle might be attacked. Oh, its not much of a castle, a little more than a tower and there were none to defend it. I thought she would be safer in the woods so I wrapped her up warm and gave her the seal to hold, as a talisman. It had been given to me long before by the Duchess Blanche, and I had cherished it for many years. Then Joseph and Becky, who served me as butler and housekeeper, took her with them to hide down by the river. I stayed behind, for I felt it my duty to try to protect the castle.'

'Couldn't your butler have done that.'

'Joseph was Becky's father,' Gida explained. 'They were Jews, and I knew it would go hard with them if they were caught. As it was I sent them unwittingly to their deaths, I went down to the woods in the morning, and found their bodies. The peasants had bypassed the castle and gone into the woods. Perhaps they wanted to rest before they continued their march to London and fell upon them by accident. But Joseph and Becky were both dead, and Diana was gone. I've never seen her since.'

'Diana?' He was frowning.

'That was her name,' Gida said. A sudden hope had dawned in her face. 'Is it possible you do know her? I made what enquiries I could, but I never heard anything. I always prayed that the peasants had taken her with them, for she was such a pretty child.'

'I knew a girl called Diana once,' Giles said, 'but she came from Devon. I say 'knew', but I only met her briefly. Her parents were lodging in a house near to the Todmores. That was before Enid and Peter were wed, and Peter brought her to meet us. We went to see the lions in the Tower'

'What was her other name?' Gida asked.

'Maundy — yes, that was it. Diana Maundy. Her parents came to visit us, to offer condolences, when my father was killed. That was a strange and tragic matter, that they should offer condolences when they were within hours of their own death. Excuse me, but I hear my sister below!'

He hurried to the door and called cheerfully down the stairs. A few moments later a pleasant faced young woman bustled in with a soberly garbed gentleman behind her.

'I brought supper for us,' she announced, depositing a covered basket on the table. 'I shall be heartily relieved when you find yourself a wife and then I can be sure you will eat well everyday of the week. Oh, but you have a visitor!'

'This is Mistress Gida Falcon, an old friend of father's,' Giles said. 'She has travelled from Kent to look for a girl called Diana. I was just telling her about Diana Maundy.'

'That was a terrible business,' Peter Todmore said, shaking hands as he was introduced.

'What happened?' Gida asked tensely.

'It was at the time of Master Aston's death,' Peter said. 'I had ridden to Oxford to tell Mistress Aston the sad news and then ridden back, and I must confess I was so tired that next night that I went to bed as soon as I had eaten. I was woken later by the Maundy's maid.'

'A rather stupid girl, wasn't she, dear?,' Enid said, beginning to lay the table.

'Half out of her mind with fear,' he corrected. 'She came hammering at the door, screaming out that her master and mistress had been killed. We could get no sense out her, and then she fell into a kind of frenzy crying out that she was feared to tell. We went round to the house and found the Maundys. There'd been a struggle of some kind, that much was certain. Mistress Maundy had fallen against the hearth and cracked her skull, and Master Maundy had been stabbed.'

'And Diana?' Gida whispered the name.

'There was no sign of her. The maid said she'd gone out earlier alone. There was a search made but she was never found.'

'And the murderer?'

'Jane declared that Diana had become betrothed to a man older than herself, that he had come back with the Maundy's that evening, having met them on their way back from their visit to my mother. She'd heard quarrelling and run to see what was wrong. She said Sir Godwin was struggling with Master Maundy — '

'Sir Godwin?' Her voice was sharp and the colour had drained from her face.

'Sir Godwin de Faucon was the man to whom Diana Maundy was betrothed,' Peter said. 'There was a warrant put out for his arrest.'

'Was he found?'

'Why, he came in of his own accord a couple of days later,' Peter said. 'He had a full explanation of what had happened too. It seems Mistress Diana had gone out without permission and when they arrived at the house Master Maundy began to upbraid his wife, and to accuse her of letting Diana run wild. They began to fight and Sir Godwin declared he tried to step between them. That was what the maid saw when she came into the room. Mistress Maundy had fallen against the hearth and Sir Godwin had drawn his dagger to try to frighten Master Maundy into quietness, but he ran upon it and died. Sir Godwin was cleared of all blame and went abroad again.'

'And Diana was never found?'

'She cannot have been your Diana,' Giles said, 'for she came from Devonshire.'

'It's a strange chance,' she mused.

'A coincidence,' Enid said. 'Come and eat, mistress. There's plenty for five as I generally make sufficient for Giles to heat over the day following.'

It was a tasty supper but Gida could eat little of it. This room was too full of memories, the whole house was crowded with shadows of the past.

Her mother, Alfreda, had brought her to stay here when she was little. She could recall how high and narrow the houses had been, and the pear tree in the garden under which her mother had sat. She had been glad when they had gone back to Marie Regina again, and puzzled because there was a new Abbot at the monastery there and talk of the old Abbot being burned for heresy.

Then the plague had come taking her mother and the Astons and leaving the housekeeper Dorothy, to take care of herself and Godwin and the baby Ralph. She had been fourteen when her father had sent for Godwin, and she had gone to Court to enter the service of the Duchess Blanche, and Dorothy had brought Ralph back to Cheapside. She had not seen Dorothy again until she had come to this house to bear the duke's lovechild, and fled again with poor, silly Petrella. Nobody had ever known that Petrella's child had lived, and it was clear that Ralph had kept his word and never allowed the names of Petrella or Godwin de Faucon to be mentioned again.

'You're very silent, mistress,' Giles said. 'I'm sorry not to have been of any use.'

'I was thinking about Dorothy,' she said, dragging her mind back to the present. 'Now that I'm in London I'd like to visit her grave. Your father wrote to me briefly when she died.'

'We can tell you easily how to get to the chantry,' Enid said. 'Father had a very expensive stone made for her. Will you be staying here with Giles?'

'No, I'm lodging at an inn,' she said. 'I left my bags there earlier.'

'Then we'll escort you back to the inn

when we leave,' Peter said. 'The streets are not safe after dark.'

'At least the rain has stopped,' Enid said glancing at the window. 'I never knew a wetter summer.'

'It will ruin the crops,' Gida said, trying desperately to appear her normal self.

It was foolish to go on hoping that this concidence of names was something more than chance, that there was meaning in it for her. The Diana who had vanished as a child could not possibly be the Diana who had been betrothed to Godwin. Such an alliance was too horrible to contemplate.

She sat, sipping her wine, listening to the conversation of the others. It was odd to watch these three ordinary young people and to realise they knew nothing of the violent backcloth to their affairs, and it would be cruel to darken their lives by telling them the whole truth.

'My parents lie near to Dorothy,' Giles said, when she rose to leave. 'You'll not be able to visit the chantry tonight, for it'll be too dark to see anything properly, but you'll be able to see it in the morning.'

'We'll make certain you get back safely to your lodging,' Peter assured her. 'Will you be spending some time in the city?'

'Probably not.' She had not the slightest

intention of involving any of them further in her search. 'I'm afraid I've brought back unhappy memories for you all.'

'We have forgotten much of our sorrow,' Giles said. 'Time has to move on, mistress.'

'Aye, that's true.' She looked at him, admiring the adaptability of the young. 'I hope you have better fortune with your business soon, Master Giles.'

'That's kind of you, mistress.' He helped her on with her cloak. 'I wish you a safe journey back to Kent.'

'It's twilight already.' Enid sounded slightly nervous. 'I think we ought to be on our way.'

'I'll see to the clearing up,' Giles said, 'Take care of yourself until next week.'

He shook hands with Peter and kissed his sister on the cheek. To Gida he said, 'We must keep in touch now that we have met at last. I would like to know how your search ends.'

'I will write to you,' she said not meaning it. He came down with them while Peter went to the stables for the horses, and in a mood of impulsive pity Gida bought a roll of vivid red cloth, firmly refusing Giles' offer to make her a gift of it. The colour was far too bright for her and the price too high, but if she ever found Diana the colour might suit the child. Child! She smiled ruefully at her own stupidity, for Diana was no longer a child. If she still lived she would be a woman grown, and her fair hair might have dimmed. If she still lived —

'Ride safely,' Giles said, helping her to the saddle.

She lifted her hand and rode with the Todmores down the long thoroughfare she had once known so well. Everything looked dirtier and smaller now and the greyish yellow pall of smoke that hung over the rooftops smelled vile.

'We are going to get a house in the country as soon as Peter has made sufficient money,' Enid said, noting Gida's look of distaste. 'It is becoming impossible to breathe in the city now that every house has its own coal fire.'

'We still use wood in Kent,' Gida said.

'I would like to visit the country,' Enid said. 'We go to Chelsea sometimes and eat food in the open, but this summer has been so wet we've had little opportunity.'

'Have you a family?' Gida asked, but the other shook her head.

'We've buried two,' she said sadly. 'Of course, we're both still young, but it was a grief to us.'

'And in a sense, I have lost two children as well,' Gida thought.

She had taken Maudelyn to be brought up in his father's household, and though he occasionally wrote to her, he very seldom visited. She doubted if he remembered the baby Diana at all, and she had never spoken of that terrible night when the peasants had come. Some griefs and guilts had to be borne alone.

'That is the chantry where my parents and old Dorothy lie,' Enid pointed.

The iron gates were closed and the tombstones gleamed wet within. Gida smiled, repressing a shiver, and rode on with her companions. The inn where she was lodging was not many streets away and she parted from the Todmores at the door of the stable-yard, wishing them well in her heart as they turned away. Whatever unhappiness had come to the Astons through the Falcons would not be continued by her.

In the low-ceilinged bedchamber when she had disrobed she knelt, folding her hands, to pray, as she had prayed for years, that Diana might return.

12

Westminster was a sprawl of grey towers, and walls and high iron gates. Diana's impression of it was one of ordered confusion with people scurrying hither and thither, others idling, a constant buzz of conversation somehow or other, all the work getting done.

The journey had been uneventful, and, as the years in the cloister had disciplined her tongue, Diana was able to resist the temptation to chatter to Master Descant. It would be as well for her to keep her own counsel, she reasoned, until she was certain that it was safe to speak out. For all she knew Godwin de Faucon had been captured and executed years before.

Within the palace she dismounted and was led through a series or rooms, none of which she remembered or recognised, into a large apartment where a bright fire defied the elements outside. There were several ladies at their tapestry frames and a page strummed a lute in one corner. For one moment Diana stood shyly, watching them, admiring their brilliantly embroidered gowns and dainty headdresses. Then a tall, plump lady who sat apart from the rest rose and beckoned her forward.

'Come with me, mistress,' she said in so cordial and pleasant a tone that it took Diana a moment to realise that this was Queen Joanna herself. The king's new wife wore a loose gown of cream velvet over a petticoat of dark red silk. Her light brown hair, in defiance of prevailing fashion, hung loosely over her shoulders and her crown was studded with rubies and diamonds which matched the heavy necklace about her neck.

She led Diana to an inner chamber and closed the door. This room was a smaller apartment with a chair set upon a dais. The queen seated herself and motioned Diana to a stool. She spoke in faintly accented English, her grey eyes fixed on Diana as if she were learning her face be heart.

'You came with Master Descant from the Convent of St Clare?'

'Yes, Your Grace.'

'And what is your name?'

'Diana Maundy, Your Grace.'

'Diana,' the queen repeated and smiled as if at some private amusement. 'That's a curious name. What's your history?'

'I was reared in Devonshire, and when I

lost my parents at eighteen, I entered the convent.'

'How old are you now?'

'Near twenty-six, Your Grace.'

'And have not taken your vows? Why?'

'The Prioress believed I was more suited to a life outside the cloister.'

'To marriage perhaps? Take off your cloak and hood and let me see you properly,' the queen ordered.

Diana did as she was told, turning slowly about, aware of the steady blue eyes fixed upon her.

'You're a comely woman,' the queen observed. 'The Prioress was right. You ought to be wed, with children about your skirts, not locked in a cloister. Have you never had a lover?'

Diana's face crimsoned and the other laughed softly.

'You need not tell me. I was never one to pry,' she said. 'I can promise that if your fancy lights upon a gentleman at Court, and he is unattached, then I will help you to a marriage, and provide you with a good dowry.'

'Your Grace is very kind,' Diana said in bewilderment.

'I was married against my will to my first husband,' the queen told her. 'He was older than I was and of most uncertain temper, but I was a loyal wife, bearing him seven children, making his concerns my concerns. Well, he died and this new marriage is to my liking. But there are too many women forced into loveless unions or locked up in convents because they lack dowry. It is my pleasure to help a few of these now that I have the power to do so.'

If the queen was mad then it was a madness of which Diana approved. This pleasant woman with the tranquil manner and the searching gaze was someone in whom she felt an instinctive trust.

'I shall expect you to wait upon me in my apartments,' she was continuing. 'Do you read and write?'

'Yes, of course,' Diana spoke with slight indignation.

'I'm glad to see that life in the cloister has not entirely subdued your pride,' the queen said.

'I was given a good education, Your Grace,' Diana said.

'And are discreet and loyal?' Again the eyes were searching.

'You may test me in those virtues any time you choose,' Diana said, lifting her chin.

'Oh, tests will come in the normal course

of events,' the queen assured her. 'Do you sing or dance?'

'I dance a little,' Diana said, 'and I used to sing sometimes when I was out in the garden at the farm where I was reared.'

'Yes. You do look a child of flowers and sunshine,' the queen said. 'I am fond of gardens myself. By moonlight a garden can be the most magical place on earth. And to walk in such a garden brings strange thoughts into the mind! But you will learn more of that if you serve me well, mistress.'

'I give you my word,' Diana said simply, and the queen nodded as if she had found something in her new attendant that pleased her.

'You will need new gowns,' she said.

'I do have a blue dress,' Diana began.

'Fashions have changed these past years,' the queen said. 'Gowns have lower waists and rounder skirts now, and headdresses are wider. We will see the dressmaker. Now you must come and meet the other ladies. Some of them came with me from Navarre, and others, like yourself, are from the cloister. You will enjoy their company.'

She rose and stepped down from the dais, beckoning to Diana to follow her again. This time they went through another door, along a winding passage and up a flight of steps into a long, low apartment with several beds curtained in silk, and an elderly woman sewing by the fire.

'Matilde, this is Diana, another of our circle,' the queen said. 'Show her where she is to sleep, and then let her meet her companions.'

'Mistress Diana, this will be your bed,' Matilde pointed to one at the end. 'Your Grace, is she to have new dresses?'

'Yes, indeed. See Mistress Lake about it.' The queen smiled at them both and went slowly out.

'She is very kind,' Diana said, watching the gracefully retreating figure.

'Very kind,' Matilde agreed. There was an odd note in her voice and the glance she shot at Diana was amused. Then she said briskly. 'Come with me, child, and you can meet the others.'

It was, Diana discovered, a strangely feminine Court. The king and his son were in Wales chasing the rebel Glendower over his mountain passes and many of the courtiers were with them so that at Westminster there was a preponderance of ladies.

'Like a beehive,' said Mistress Anne.

She was a distractingly pretty girl with light, silvery hair and round blue eyes that bore an expression of continual surprise. Like

Diana she had been plucked from the cloister where, she confided, her jealous mother had placed her because she feared rivalry.

'In Joanna of Navarre's Court all the women are queens,' she said mysteriously.

'How so?' Diana asked with interest.

'As to that you will see tonight,' Anne said. 'It is Midsummer Eve, or had you forgotten?'

She had forgotten. In the convent, season followed season with nothing to mark them save the feasts of the church when there was usually an extra ration of bread. But in Devon they had celebrated midsummer, dancing and drinking ale and crowning one of the farm girls with poppies and young corn. Diana turned away that the other might not see the glint of tears in her eyes.

She had been nearly two weeks at Court and was beginning to find her way round the vast maze of the palace. It was a warren of rooms, passages, stairways and courtyards, with a throng of people forever passing to and fro. Her duties were very light for the queen disliked energetic exercise and spent much of her time listening to music or sewing in her apartments or in one of the many bower gardens enclosed within the high walls.

'There will be dancing tonight,' Anne promised her. 'Some of the young gentlemen have returned from Ireland, and so we will have partners.'

'Ireland?' Diana spoke casually but her heart had jerked.

'And afterwards we will have the ring game,' Anne continued.

'What's that?' Diana enquired, but the other girl only laughed telling her it was an invention of the queen's and she must wait and see.

Midsummer or not it was raining and cool, a fact that seemed to irritate Joanna very much.

'The ceremonies are not so effective held within doors,' she complained.

'Ceremonies?' Diana who was dressing the long brown hair into a series of elaborate ringlets looked curious.

'To the Great Mother,' the queen said. 'She who is older by far than the god of the Christians. Have you never heard of her, child?'

'I've heard of Our Lady,' Diana said doubtfully.

'Ah, sweet Mary Virgin, the most perfect daughter the Great Mother ever bore!' Joanna exclaimed. 'Men deny the Goddess, you know, reducing women to chattels, setting themselves up as kings of creation. They try to forget that we hold the power of life and death in our hands, for man must be born of woman and as he was made in the image of God so God sprang from the Great Mother.'

'It sounds like heresy,' Diana said uneasily.

'Some would call it so. Others are wiser.' The queen waved her away and took a satisfied look at her reflection. 'Tonight, in the dance, I represent the Great Mother and my attendants are aspects of myself. Will you be Diana who tears men to pieces with her hounds, or will you be Diana, the many breasted, who nourishes them?'

'Your Grace, how can I tell?' Diana asked in bewilderment.

'The young men will be there,' Joanna said. 'It will be for you to choose or reject.'

Perhaps she was a little mad after all, Diana thought, but it seemed a kindly madness.

Her new gown was laid across the end of her bed when she returned to the dormitory. Mistress Lake had worked fast and to good effect. The silver grey gown was embroidered with tiny flowers of blue and silver, the hanging sleeves lined with black velvet, the shallow neckline edged with silver ribbon. The low crowned headdress was of silver tissue, bordered with blue flowers.

When she was dressed she thought, with a touch of amusement, that the good Sisters would not have recognised their erstwhile charge. The other ladies were attired in equally charming gowns, but even the prettiest was eclipsed by the queen. In contrast to her ladies she wore a severely cut gown of black velvet with enormous sleeves of white silk gathered at the wrists with gold thread. Leaves fashioned from pearls and emeralds decorated her curled head and her cloak was cloth of gold.

'We will dance the ring dance first,' Anne said to Diana. 'Then, when we have our partners, we give wine and fruit to the Great Mother. You understand that this is a private entertainment not to be spoken about in Open Court?'

Diana nodded, wondering if Open Court included the king. He was said to be a good churchman who would disapprove surely of the amusements his charming bride enjoyed during his absence.

'Does she not fear gossip?' she whispered.

'From her ladies? Why, we are bound to her by gratitude,' Anne said primly. 'And would you exchange these revels for long years back in the cloister?'

Diana shook her head. Something that had once blossomed in her youth was wakening into life again, and she was in no mood to deny it.

A galleried chamber had been set apart and Joanna's own personal guards stood at the doors. Diana, entering with the others, had a confused impression of many candles surrounding the figure clad in black and gold, of a long table laid with platters of food and jugs of wine, of young men in black face masks, of throbbing music and the heavy scent of musk.

Then she was circling with her companions, facing inwards, while the masked men facing outwards moved in the contrary direction. And in the centre the queen sat motionless, her mouth smiling, her blue eyes intent. The music was faster now and they were whirling, like stars about the sun. She closed her eyes dizzily, but the candles still shone behind her eyelids and the perfume swirled about her, drugging her senses.

The dance ended so abruptly that she almost fell. Each lady turned, each man turned, removing his mask. Diana stared into narrow, brilliantly green eyes, set in a long face framed in yellow hair. His voice was as she remembered it, quick and light, trembling on the edge of laughter.

'Mistress Maundy, I bid you welcome after long years!'

'Master Falcon!' Her voice was only a

thread of sound and his face blurred suddenly.

'Come and sit down.' He led her out of the circle to a low couch. 'It has given you too much of a shock.'

'You knew I would be here?'

'Not until a few moments ago when Her Grace chanced to mention your name.'

'I didn't know you were at Court,' she said faintly.

'Some of us returned only a few hours ago. I had no wish to miss the revels.'

'You knew about them?'

'They were a feature of life in Navarre,' he told her.

'I thought you were in Ireland.'

'Ireland, France, Spain — I've been in all those countries,' he said. 'And in all these years I've had no word of you.'

'Did you ask after me?'

'I meant to ask,' he said, laughing a little. 'I truly meant to ask, but time goes so quickly and my duties have kept me occupied.'

'Are you still running errands?' she asked with a touch of malice.

'Always on the move,' he said with an exaggerated sigh.

'Then you never settled?'

'I believe I was born with wings on my

'heels,' he said. 'But where have you been this age?'

'In a convent,' she said demurely.

'In a — ?' He stared at her for a moment and then laughed. 'So you are one of Her Grace's convent waifs!' he exclaimed. 'She had them in Navarre too, and many of them made good marriages. But what happened to your parents? And the betrothal that you mentioned?'

'My parents died and the betrothal came to nothing,' she said.

'And so you are at the Court of Queen Joanna? Are you happy here?'

'I am now,' she said simply, and felt the loneliness of the years fall away.

'Then we must sacrifice to the Great Mother!' he cried and, taking her hand, pulled her to her feet. 'We'll drink wine and eat the honey cakes to honour her and the blessings she brings!'

'Is it not heresy?' she asked, but her question was lost in laughter and the stamping of feet as the young men and women ran to take food and drink from the table while others continued to dance, not circling now, but twined in couples in a measure that was more like an embrace.

They drank from the same cup with arms entwined, and ate the honey cake, sprinkling dregs and crumbs in a deep dish at the feet of the queen, and then danced again, slowly, lingeringly, the music and the perfume dreaming around them.

'You are more beautiful than you used to be,' Maudelyn told her.

'And you are — more yourself,' she said softly.

'We met in church,' he began, then stopped, surprise on his face. 'Lord, but I must have met a hundred maids,' he said, 'Yet I can recall where we met! Is that an omen?'

'A fortunate one,' she said boldly.

'It is as if I recognised you this time more fully than I did before,' he said pensively. 'Are you sure you've woven no spell to entrap me? They say that the queen, at her private entertainments, spices the wine with certain herbs that heat a man's blood and send his desires soaring.'

'We drank from the same goblet,' Diana pointed out.

'Then you must feel as I do. Tell me how you feel?'

'Like sun and moon crushing together and turning into millions of stars,' she murmured. 'Like a green plant pushing through the earth, or a river running fast to the sea.'

'We waste time in talking,' he said, and

she followed his gaze, her eyes widening, for most had ceased to dance and were sinking to the floor, limbs bared, eyes half closed, mouths panting. Each pair seemed oblivious of those around them, and the queen stood still in the centre of the room, watching with smiling mouth.

'Is it not sinful?' Diana said, but she asked almost lazily, for it seemed that nothing real existed outside this perfumed, candlelit apartment.

'It is your choice,' he said, 'and I'll not force you. I never forced a maid.'

The queen was still watching, sly wisdom in her face.

Diana moved towards her, drawn by that compelling blue gaze and heard her own voice, raised in tremulous question.

'Your Grace, what shall I do?'

'This is the gift of the Great Mother,' Joanna said. 'Not a loveless union for the sake of position or property, not vows mouthed in a cold church, but flesh offering flesh in the renewal of joy. But it is always the woman's choice, for in my Court women are the stronger.'

'To hunt with hounds or be many-breasted,' Diana said.

'It is your choice,' Joanna said.

'While you look on?'

'Would you deny your queen a little pleasure?' Joanna arched an eyebrow, her mouth still smiling. 'For me there is great pleasure in watching the pleasure of others. It was a habit of my father's too.'

She was truly strange, Diana thought, trying to turn the world on its head to fulfil her own desires.

'We can go up into the gallery where it is most private,' Maudelyn said at her elbow.

She was never sure afterwards what she had replied. Perhaps she had said nothing at all, because he had slipped his arm around her waist and was leading her towards the stairs. If she had had any thoughts of resistance they faded like dew in sunshine as she leaned against the strength of his arm. He was as slender as he had been in boyhood, but the years had hardened him, imparting a new authority, a lithe grace to his whipcord frame.

There were low pallets laid along the gallery, piled with bright cushions and woven covers. Some were already occupied, but the lighting here was very dim and she could see nothing and nobody clearly.

'Dear Mistress Diana!' He had drawn her down to one of the pallets and was holding her so closely that she was not certain if she could feel his heart or her own beating.

There were so many questions she wanted to ask him. They flashed through her mind and were lost in his kissing. Her gown slipped from her shoulders and his hands tugged at her headdress. There was music again, sweet enough to draw her soul out of her body, and her hair falling about her face and curling at her temples, and his green eyes in which she saw herself for an instant small and gleaming and then the sound of his own panting breath. She had become the earth in which the green plant thrust itself, and her whole universe was made of stars.

The queen moved out of the centre of the room below and helped herself to wine. She wished it had been a fine evening when they could have danced on the grass and lain under the night sky, but her own apartments were probably safer. It was unlikely that any of her household would chatter to the king, and if they did she was confident she could divert any suspicions he might have. Her stepson was a different matter. Henry of Monmouth had already shown himself to be less than friendly to his father's new wife, and he was a devout Christian with no sympathy for unconventional ideas.

Sipping her wine she leaned against a pillar and watched with increasing pleasure as the candlelit figures writhed and moaned in the ecstasy of their fulfilment. At these times she felt truly a goddess.

13

Gida had slept badly and woke early. The inn was clean and the bed had been comfortable, but she had tossed and turned restlessly all night. Perhaps, after all, she had been a fool to come. Her instinct to delay had been a sound one, and it was still not too late. She could ride back to Marie Regina this very day and forget every dream she had ever had of finding Diana. There was little likelihood now of the girl being alive. Perhaps it was as well, for at least if she were dead she would have avoided the horror of being married to Godwin. It was so many years since she had seen her brother that she wondered if she would even recognise him if they met. They had never been close even as children, and the only time they had met in adult life she had known, without knowing exactly how she knew, that Godwin was the kind of man who caused pain to people. Now, remembering the garbled tale about the Maundy's, Gida wondered, with a clutch of fear, if her brother had killed them. It seemed a terrible thing to believe of a brother, but the suspicion had gripped her and would not let loose.

Almost against her will she found herself, later that morning, making her way through the iron gates that Peter Todmore had pointed out to her the previous night. They stood open now and she walked slowly between the tombstones up to the porch.

The chantry was larger within than it appeared from the outside. Gida walked round, reading the memorial plaques set into the walls above the candlesconces, dreading to find by some terrible mischance, the name of Diana Maundy. Dorothy's tomb was a handsome one, gilded and carved with angels and skulls.

Gida stared down at it, thinking how Dorothy would hate such grandeur. She had been a sensible, bustling woman who had devoted her life to her charges, never blaming or questioning them, but always there in the background whenever she was needed. She had been middle-aged when she had left Marie Regina and come to London, and she had never returned. It seemed hard that she should lie here under cold stone. At least she was close to Ralph Aston and his wife whose equally ornate tomb was only a few feet away.

She murmured a brief prayer and continued to walk round the chantry. There were side aisles leading to a Lady Chapel and to a shrine dedicated to St Raphael. At this second altar she paused, looking up at the brightly painted statue with its sweeping wings of blue and gold. Raphael had always been her favourite archangel, the one to whom she always prayed before she pounded herbs for medicines. She had taught Diana to pray to St Raphael too. The child had folded her slim hands and repeated the words after her.

'Good-morrow, mistress. I fear you come too late for Mass.'

A small bent priest stood behind her, his manner mildly enquiring.

'I came to pay my respects at the tomb of some old friends of mine,' she said.

'Buried here?'

'The Astons. Master Ralph Aston was killed some years ago.'

'I remember it,' the priest said. 'Murdered by footpads, was he not?'

'And the killer never found.'

'Very sad,' he said. 'I knew Master Aston slightly when he was alive. He used to come here occasionally. His old nurse lies here too.'

'I suppose you know the name on every memorial plaque in this church,' she said.

'Some of them, not all.'

'There wouldn't be — ' She hesitated, then

rushed on. 'There wouldn't be a Maundy buried here?'

'Maundy. Maundy.'

'Diana Maundy.' There were a hundred chantries in the city and no possible guarantee that Diana, were she dead, had been buried here. Yet she waited for the answer in an agony of suspense.

'There is an Alice Maundy,' he said at last. 'A child who was buried here more than twenty years ago. I remember the name now.'

'Why now?' Gida asked sharply.

'Some years ago, seven or eight, a young lady came here to enquire about an Alice Maundy. She wished to know all about the child.'

'What did you tell her?'

'Well, I had to look her up in the registers,' he said. 'I was not present when the little girl died. It was in the year of the peasants' rebellion, and I was then attached to another parish. The child died of smallpox.'

'Smallpox!'

'Her parents were from Devonshire, here on a visit. They left money for Masses for her soul.'

'And another girl came to ask questions?'

'It was my Diana,' she thought with a flash of joyful certainty. 'The peasants brought her with them when they marched upon London, and somehow or other this couple who had lost their child took Diana in her place.'

'A fair-haired maid,' the priest said 'I recall her because she seemed so distressed. Odd really!'

'What was odd?'

'That two such maids should come seeking help.'

'Two?'

'Father Christopher was here the second time. He told us about it at recreation. A young woman sought sanctuary here. He took her to the Abbot of course.'

'And from there?'

'To a convent. She could hardly remain here.'

'Which one?'

She must have spoken too eagerly, for a slight frown creased his brow.

'Why do you ask?'

'I knew the Maundys,' she evaded.

'Oh, this girl was no relation,' he assured her. 'Father Christopher said that she was dressed like a — like a light woman. I believe the Abbot took her to the Convent of St Clare. 'Tis beyond Windsor — almost a day's ride off.'

'Did the maid give her name?'

'Not that we heard. I only remember it

because the two events occurred within a week or two of each other. It is not often that we see pretty young ladies in his place. The young don't frequent buildings dedicated to death.'

'Nor the old, if they can help it,' she said crisply. 'I thank you for your help, Father. Will you accept this contribution to the Mass?'

'With pleasure, mistress.' He accepted the gold coin with a tactful lack of eagerness. 'I shall pray for you and for your departed.'

'Pray for the living too,' she said, and took another look at the statue of the archangel before she left.

At the inn, after a little bargaining, Gilda was able to obtain the services of an escort, a squinting man whose empty sleeve hinted at war service.

'I was reared near St Clare's,' he told her. 'It's a small House, but very straitly kept.'

'Is there accommodation there for the night?' she wanted to know.

'There's an inn a mile or so, down the road,' he said, scratching his head. 'You can stay there, mistress.'

'That will do.' She nodded at him pleasantly, striving to contain her excitement.

It was possible that the girl who had gone asking questions at the chantry was the same one who had fled there for sanctuary. And if it had been Diana then it was likely that she knew about the deaths of the couple who had brought her up. It was useless trying to tell herself that she might be on a fool's errand. After so many years she was certain that her search was coming to an end. It was with difficulty that she restrained her eager impatience and maintained an even trot along the mud splashed lanes.

It being September there were many passing and repassing on the Windsor roads, for the season of visiting was drawing to its close and the winter threatened already in the grey clouds and biting wind. If it was not Diana who was at the convent then she would return to London, find out where the Maundys had lodged and where their Devonshire home had been. If necessary she would travel during the winter. She had come alone from Kent and she was capable of finding her way into Devonshire.

They broke their fast at noon in a roadside tavern where the wine was sour and the bread too salty, but she wouldn't have noticed if the wine had been mellow and the bread sweet. She had not even realised that it had started to rain again; fine, steady rain soaking through her cloak and making her joints creak in protest. As the miles stretched out behind her so she felt the years slip away too. She was no longer a greying woman past fifty, but a vigorous young woman in search of the child she had lost only the day before.

'That is the convent of St Clare, mistress,' her guide pointed.

A high wooden gate set between stone walls was ahead of them. Her escort spurred on to ring the bell.

'The extern Sister will take your name. I'll ride on to the inn and find a night's lodgings for us, mistress,' he said.

A panel slid sideways in the gate and an eye appeared.

'Mistress Gida Falcon to see the Prioress,' Gida said loudly.

The eye withdrew, the panel slid into place, and the gate was pulled back.

She dismounted in a cobbled yard and followed the nun along a stone passage and up a flight of steps into a small, chilly parlour. Gida took the stool that the other indicated and waited patiently.

There was the rattle of rings as the leather blind was raised and behind the grille was a tall, veiled figure.

'Deo Gratia. Mistress Gida Falcon, is it not?' Her voice was clear, with the habit of authority in it.

'I am grateful to you for seeing me, Mother Prioress,' Gida said.

'Have you travelled a long way? Your garments are wet,' the Prioress asked.

'From London today. I was anxious to be here and didn't notice the rain.'

'It has been a very wet year,' the Prioress agreed. 'I fear we have no accommodation for visitors, but our extern Sister will see that you have food and dry your cloak.'

'My guide is arranging lodging for me at the inn.'

'A respectable place and moderately clean.' The Prioress seated herself, folding her hands, and spoke briskly. 'What brings you to St Clare? How may we help you?'

'I am searching for a girl, a young woman,' Gida said hesitantly.

'A Sister?'

'I don't know. This young woman left her home several years ago. My information is that she was brought to this convent after seeking sanctuary at a chantry in London.'

'Many young women come into convents,' the Prioress said. 'What is her name?'

'Diana. She was known as Diana Maundy.'

There was such a long pause that she feared that the other was not going to answer. Then the Prioress said, frowning down at her hands, 'You must understand, mistress, that when a young woman enters a cloister she renounces her earthly life. We become dead to the world, riches and earthly desires laid aside. I may know the history of my nuns, but I do not reveal them.'

'Diana was — in my charge when she was a child,' Gida pleaded.

'There was a Diana Maundy here,' the Prioress said slowly.

'Was?'

'Mistress Falcon, I have to tell you that she is — no longer with us,' the other said.

'Dead?' She heard her own voice pronounce the word dully.

'It would be better for you to return home,' the Prioress said. Her voice was not unkind but it was firm, admitting of no argument. 'I regret that your journey has been fruitless, mistress.'

It was a journey that had started more than twenty years before, Gida thought sadly, and now it was over. Diana had died here in this quiet, grey place of grilles and stone walls. It was odd but she could not feel genuine grief, only a numb, sick sensation as if she had bitten on something sour.

'I am grateful to you for receiving me,' she said, rising and drawing her damp cloak about her. 'I will leave a contribution. Would it be possible to see where Diana lies?'

'I'm afraid that laywomen are not permitted to enter the enclosure,' the Prioress said. 'Deo Gratia.'

The blind rattled down into place again and she was alone in the parlour. It was certainly very cold, she thought shudderingly, and there was no welcome in the air. Had it been thus for Diana or had the sunny child she had once loved become a repressed and shadowy creature who accepted the limitations of the cloister?

She rose at last and went slowly down the stairs. Now, for the first time in months, she did feel her age, and there were questions still to be asked. Even if she was not permitted to enter the enclosure and pay her respects at Diana's grave, she surely had the right to know what had happened.

'I have some broth for you, mistress,' the extern Sister said as Gida reached the passage.

'It's kind of you, but I'm not hungry,' Gida said. 'I am going to the inn at once. My journey here had — a sad result, I fear.'

'Mother Prioress told me that it would be better for you to return home,' the nun said.

'I would have liked to see her grave,' Gida said wistfully.

'As to that — ' The nun said hesitating,

and bit her lip. 'I shall pray for you, Mistress Falcon,' she said, and went to open the gate.

The inn was, as the Prioress had said, respectable and moderately clean. At least there was a good fire and the supper that had been prepared was tastily spiced.

She ate, a little guilty to find she was enjoying it. Diana was dead, and yet she was enjoying her meal. There had been a time when she had been able to sense things that had happened without being told of them, but the gift had become rusty with disuse. She had had to be told of Diana's death, and even now the thought of it had an unreality which puzzled her.

'Bad weather, mistress?'

She blinked slightly as the innkeeper stopped by her table with the wine jug in his hand.

'Yes. Yes, bad weather indeed,' she said politely.

'You're from London, I hear?'

'From Kent actually.' She indicated a vacant stool, glad of the chance to talk and escape from the burden of her own thoughts. 'I've been staying in London.'

'Have you relatives at the convent?' the innkeeper enquired. 'Excuse my asking, mistress, but there are not many who visit the convent. 'Tis a strict enclosure.'

'I had a — niece there, but it seems that she has died.'

'I'm sorry to hear that, mistress. It's a sad place to die.'

'Sad?'

'Oh, very holy, I've no doubt,' he said hastily. 'It just doesn't seem natural to me, that's all, shutting up a lot of women together. It may be sinful, but I'm always glad when one leaves.'

'Does that ever happen?' she asked.

'Not very often. There was a maid rode out of there not long since, with a gentleman. Pretty thing she was, for all her nun's habit. I could see her fair curls peeping under her hood.'

'Fair?'

'Yellow as butter,' the man nodded. 'I said to myself, 'There's one who won't be taking any vows of chastity'.'

'How long ago was this?' Gida asked, sharply.

'Let me think.' He poured himself a measure of wine to help his thinking. 'It was the week my potboy went and caught his foot in a trap, and I went over to Windsor to bring back the new mare. It would be June, about the middle of the month. Yes, that's right. I remember watching them ride by and thinking to myself that it's not often you see one ride in, then ride out again.'

'You saw her ride in?'

'About — eight years ago. She wasn't in a nun's habit then, mind. She had a blue gown on, a ballgown. There was a monk with her. Oh, I'd not have seen them but she'd been taken sick on the road. Not serious, just a mite faint after the long ride. The priest brought her in here for a glass of wine before they continued on their way.'

'Did you speak to her?'

'No chance of that, mistress.' He grinned and took another swig of his wine. 'The priest made her sit by the fire and cover her gay dress with a blanket, and he gave her the wine himself. But I remember her pretty face and that yellow hair.'

'And you saw the same woman ride past this June?'

'I'd not mistake her,' he said, 'but they didn't stop this time. They rode on by.'

'They?'

'A young man in the royal livery,' the innkeeper said. 'It's my belief they were going to Court.'

'To Windsor?'

'Wherever the Court is being held,' he said. 'Of course, the king's away now fighting the Welsh, but they say that his new queen has been at Westminster all summer.'

'Westminster.' She repeated the word with an irresistible desire to laugh. So it was back to London after all, back and forth like the tide in search of one particular shell.

The Prioress had lied — or at least misled her into believing that Diana was dead. Gida was tempted to ride straight back to the convent and demand the truth, but a moment's reflection convinced her that such a course would be foolish. The Prioress must have believed that she had a good reason to behave as she did, and Gida feared that, if she went back to ask questions, then means might be found of warning Diana that a strange woman was seeking her.

She would be wiser to stay overnight in this hostelry and then ride back to Westminster. It was years since she had visited the palace, so long since that she felt for an instant as if her life was moving into a circle, her end merging into her beginning.

'I'm sorry about your niece,' the innkeeper said.

'My niece?' She looked at him vaguely for a moment and then smiled. 'Oh, I have the impression she is in good hands,' she said softly. 'I think I'll go up to my room now and get a good night's sleep in preparation for an early start.'

'We've not many guests, so you've a chamber to yourself,' he assured her. 'Your escort is in the barn loft but he's been fed and the horses watered. Is there anything else you need, mistress?'

'Nothing. Goodnight.' She bowed and went up the curving wooden staircase to the small apartment she had been given.

The moon had risen, and she gazed at it for a long time before she closed the shutters. Diana was goddess of the moon, and surely the moon protected her own.

Westminster, seen through driving rain, presented a dismal aspect. Gida had paid off her guide as soon as the towers and spires of the city came into view, and rode on alone.

At the main gates a guard enquired her name and let her pass, retreating under cover again without further enquiry. She dismounted, called to a lounging stableboy to take her horse, and went on into the complex of rooms and passages. The household Steward would have a list of those employed regularly in the palace. She needed to know if a woman called Diana Maundy was one of them. Failing that, she would have to trace the young man who had gone to the convent of St Clare the previous June. It was a daunting prospect, because so many served at Court and records were not always kept of their comings and goings.

It was an eerie sensation, walking through the apartments where she had walked as a girl. She had been fourteen years old and excited at the thought of meeting all the great Court personages of whom she had heard. She had been so very young, so certain of a bright and shining future.

'May I help you, mistress?'

A young woman had stepped forward from an alcove and was regarding her with polite curiosity.

'I am on my way to the Steward's apartment,' Gida said.

'Oh, but you are going in the wrong direction,' the girl said earnestly. 'The Steward does all his business in the east wing beyond the armoury.'

'Times change,' Gida said ruefully, 'and I forget! I have not been at Court for many years.'

'I am Madge Weston, mistress,' the girl said.

'Gida Falcon.' She clasped hands briefly. 'I used to serve at Court long ago. That was when King Edward and Queen Philippa were upon the throne.'

'I am maid in waiting to Queen Joanna,' the other informed her, 'but Her Grace went to Windsor with some of the other ladies. If you were seeking a post the Mistress of the Bedchamber is the one to help you.'

'No, not a post. I'm seeking a person. A young woman who may have been given a post here sometime in June.'

'Since the king married there have been many newcomers at Court.'

'This one's name was Diana. Diana Maundy?'

'Oh, but she was one of Her Grace's personal attendants,' Madge said promptly. 'Tall and golden-haired.'

'Was?' Gida's hand reached out and clutched at the other's sleeve. 'Was? Do you know where she is now? It is of very great importance to me.'

'Why, if you are Mistress Falcon,' the girl said, looking puzzled, 'then surely you know that already!'

14

'This is the second time in a week that you have excused yourself from attendance on Her Grace,' Mathilde scolded.

'I am not well,' Diana said. ' 'Tis something I ate, I think.'

'More likely something you did,' the old woman said. 'When were your flowers last upon you?'

'Why, seven — eight weeks ago, I think.' Diana blushed, such matters having never been openly discussed in the cloister.

'And I've no doubt your breasts hurt and you cannot face your breakfast.'

'That's true. You don't believe — ?' Diana sat down abruptly and stared at the other.

'I believe you ought to speak to the queen,' Mathilde said firmly. 'She has promised dowries to those who require them.'

'But I am — he has not offered to wed me,' Diana stammered.

'If he's taken his pleasure then he must be ready to pay,' Mathilde shrugged. 'This is a respectable Court and Her Grace will not be amused by the spectacle of her ladies dropping bastards.'

Diana was silent, but her thoughts were troubled. She was not much surprised to be told that she was pregnant, for it only confirmed her suspicions, but how Maudelyn would react she had no notion. He was an attentive lover who courted her openly with flowers and compliments, but they had never talked of marriage or even of betrothal. Indeed they had never talked of serious subjects at all.

Later that same evening she was summoned to the queen's bedchamber.

Joanna had divested herself of her stiff Court robes and was attired in a loose, velvet gown edged with miniver. Her smile was cordial but from the way her eyes flickered at once to Diana's waistline the girl knew at once why she had been called.

'Sit down, my dear,' she invited. 'Are you feeling better?'

'Thank you, Your Grace.' Diana sat down on the stool that had been placed ready for her.

'So you are with child,' Joanna said.

'I am not certain yet, Your Grace,' Diana murmured.

'Mathilde is quite certain that you are about two months gone, and she has not yet been proved wrong in such matters. It is Maudelyn Falcon, is it not?'

'There has never been anyone else,' Diana said.

'Then you must be speedily married,' Joanna said.

'But he hasn't asked me,' Diana said.

'Does he know you are with child?' Joanna asked.

'No, Your Grace.'

'Then he will have to be told and a date for the ceremony set. I promised a dowry for any of my ladies who wished to wed. I will settle three hundred pounds upon you.'

'But he may not wish — Your Grace, I believe that he loves me, but he has always made it clear that he never wanted to settle down and marry.'

'He's not unusual in that. Most men have to be persuaded into marriage, but they don't find it too harsh a condition once the vows are exchanged.'

'Your Grace, I don't know who my parents are,' Diana blurted out. 'I was reared by kind people who had lost their own daughter, but they died and I entered the cloister. I don't know my real name or my family. I might be a bastard.'

'As Maudelyn is,' Joanna said. 'He is not ashamed of his beginnings.'

'He is the son of a duke. That makes a difference.'

'And you may be the daughter of a duchess. These are foolish excuses. You do love your young man?'

'Oh, yes!' Diana's blue eyes glowed.

'And I am certain he loves you,' Joanna said. 'We will send for him tomorrow and inform him that he is to be a bridegroom as well as a lover. I warrant he'll be delighted.'

'Yes, Your Grace.' Diana spoke meekly, but her eyes were troubled.

'Men require to be gentled into marriage,' Joanna said. 'Listen to me, child. Those who are invited to my private ceremonies know that they must keep silent about what happened there, and they also understand that if a child results then there must be marriage. Maudelyn was aware of that from the beginning, and still he chose you as his companion, and you chose to be the many-breasted and not she who tears her suitor to pieces. You both had free choice and the Goddess has blessed you with seed. It must grow within the security of a marriage.'

'Yes, Your Grace.' She rose and curtsied respectfully.

'I am going to Windsor in a week or two,' the queen said. 'We will probably winter there and wait for His Grace to return from Wales. He is leaving Prince Henry there to strike camp and hold the ground we have gained in that land, but some of the men-at-arms and the older knights will be returning with the king. They cannot be expected to endure the rigours of a Welsh winter.'

'Will the younger men have to go to the Welsh camp?' Diana said uneasily.

'It's likely,' the queen gave her an amused glance and said. 'As soon as you are wed I shall instruct Master Falcon to take you into the country and to remain with you until after the child is born.'

'You're very kind,' Diana said gratefully.

'It is one of my few virtues,' Joanna said wryly. 'Sleep well, child.'

But sleep was elusive. Dreams, that ended always with a circle of grinning faces and a child's voice calling, 'Becky,' woke her frequently, and dawn found her heavy eyed and listless. Mathilde, after one look at her face, ordered her to stay abed until noon.

'For it's still raining, and there is nothing important happening today. Her Grace had business to attend this morning, so I will bring you a tisane and you must try to rest,' she said. 'Now try to sleep and get some colour back into your cheeks.'

Having a child was a dreadful business, Diana thought miserably, pummelling her pillow. She was quite determined after this one she would do her best not to have any more.

'Diana, Mistress Diana! Why didn't you tell me the news?'

'Mistress Anne?' Diana sat up as the other came into the dormitory.

'I thought we were friends,' Anne reproached, 'and now you are to be married this very day, and you lie there in bed and keep absolutely mute about it.'

'Today?' But who — ?'

'I met Master Maudelyn on his way from the queen's apartment,' Anne said, flouncing down on the edge of the bed. 'He said I was to wish him joy because he and Mistress Maundy were to be married this very afternoon. Her Grace is giving you one of her gowns for the ceremony for you are much the same height though she is plumper. But you cannot possibly lie there. Do get up and tell me all about it. Has he given you a betrothal ring?'

'I don't like betrothal rings,' Diana interrupted.

'You're a strange young woman!' Anne exclaimed. 'But there, I don't suppose it matters if you love the man. You do, don't you?'

'Very much,' Diana said softly.

'And 'tis certain that he loves you,' Anne

said. 'Why, he has paid you such loving attention since Midsummer Eve that you cannot doubt it! I never saw anybody so taken with a maid before.'

'Yes,' Diana forced certainty into her voice. At least Maudelyn had agreed, and marriage was probably, as Joanna had said, a condition into which men had to be persuaded.

The queen had sent over a loose robe of parchment silk bound under the bust with narrow scarlet ribbon. Anne and Madge dressed her hair in long ringlets, binding each curl with scarlet ribbon and laying a veil of fine lace over her head. Mathilde had made her swallow some bread and fruit, and someone else put a spray of dark red roses in her hand.

Then she was walking into the queen's private chapel. It was a small, richly decorated apartment lit by clusters of candles and perfumed now by the incense rising from the thurible.

She had a brief glimpse of Maudelyn, standing tall and slim in a short gown of scarlet silk bound with gold, then the priest stepped forward, and she heard her own voice answering him and Maudelyn's deeper tones. It was not the wedding of which she had dreamed, but it was beautiful. She knew that, without any shadow of doubt, when Maudelyn put the wide gold band upon her finger, and gave her a comforting, little nod as if to reassure her that it hadn't taken much persuasion to get him to this marriage after all.

'We have no bride cake,' the queen said, kissing her as they came out into the State Apartment again. 'It took me much trouble to procure a special licence. Master Maudelyn rushed off to buy the ring himself, and then rushed back. I tell you, child, we have none of us known if we were on our heads or our heels these last few hours.'

'She gave him no opportunity to change his mind,' Diana thought, then wisely pushed the thought away.

Maudelyn looked happy and it was her task to ensure that he remained so and never regretted the wedding.

'I am taking you to my mother's home in Kent,' Maudelyn told her as they sipped wine in the corner. 'You'll like my mother. It's some years since I was last at home but I write to her from time to time.'

'Will she be angry at your having married?'

'Angry? Not her! My mother has been hinting for years that it's time I gave her grandchildren,' Maudelyn said.

'As to that — ' She bit her lip, meeting

his eyes with painful honesty.

'I know.' He gave her a grave, tender glance. 'Her grace told me about the child.'

'I would have told you myself, but I didn't want you to feel obliged to wed me,' she whispered.

'You forget that I am a bastard,' he said. 'Oh, they say bastards ought not to feel shame at what is not their own fault, and Lord knows the Duke of Lancaster had many bastards running about in his household and he loved them as much as he loved his trueborn children. But there was a difference all the same, something bred in the bone, I think. No child of mine will be born out of wedlock.'

So he married her for the sake of the babe. Yet he looked at her with love and she would build on that.

'Your bags are packed and your horses saddled,' the queen said, rustling across. 'Diana, a word with you!'

'Your Grace?'

They walked into the long antechamber and here Joanna handed Diana a small bag.

'Your dowry, Mistress Falcon,' she said smilingly, 'I did not neglect my promise.'

'Your Grace has been most kind,' Diana said.

'I like to see a young woman gain her

heart's desire,' Joanna said simply, 'and sometimes, with the help of the Goddess, I am able to help her to it. You will not speak of what you have seen?'

'No, Your Grace.'

'Men rule now,' Joanna said, 'making us chattels, forcing us into convents, but the Goddess does not forsake her daughters, and the time will come when we will show our strength, and men will realise we are not creatures to be used, but hold life and death in our hands. God go with you, Mistress Diana!'

She was undoubtedly a little mad, Diana thought in bewilderment.

A pale ray of sunshine lighted the sky as they mounted in the courtyard. Diana was muffled in her cloak and threw her roses to Anne, who caught them, calling that she would send an invitation to the wedding when she had hunted down a bridegroom.

The laughter of friends was heart-warming, Diana thought. Since the morning she had heard the news of her parents' deaths there had been little gaiety in her life.

They rode but a short distance in the teeming rain before stopping at the inn where Maudelyn had hired a lodging for the night. It gave Diana a strange, trembling sensation to touch the gold ring on her finger. It was the visible symbol of her hasty marriage that she was determined would succeed.

'We'll make our way by easy stages,' Maudelyn said, looking with some concern at her white face when they rose in the morning. 'No sense in risking a miscarriage.'

'It was the excitement,' she said apologetically, 'everything was done in such haste.'

'When Queen Joanna gets an idea in her head she doesn't rest until it is accomplished,' Maudelyn agreed.

'And she gave me a handsome dowry,' Diana handed him the bag of coins.

'We'll spend it on the child,' he said confidently. 'You'll not mind sharing the house with my mother. She's a good woman for all that she bore me out of wedlock. I believe the only man she ever loved was John of Gaunt, but to him she was a passing pleasure, no more.'

'As I would have been to you,' Diana thought, 'if the queen had not hurried matters on.'

The journey, despite the rain, was less uncomfortable than she had feared. Every hour took them further from the smoky city and deeper into meadow and woodland. The year was moving into a wet and windless September, and there were many travellers on the roads hurrying back from summer visits before the winter set in.

'We reach Marie Regina tomorrow,' Maudelyn told her as they prepared for bed one evening.

He was divesting himself of his hose and didn't notice the slight start she gave.

'Marie Regina?' Diana pronounced the words carefully, sitting up in bed with her hair about her shoulders.

' 'Tis the name of the castle. Surely I told you?'

'No,' she said carefully. 'No, you did not.'

'I scarcely remember it myself,' he said, 'for my mother took me to Kenilworth when I was a little lad to be brought up by my natural father. She doesn't own the place. It was a hunting lodge at one time but she was born there. Of course her parents are long dead now.'

'Falcons,' Diana said.

'Originally I believe it was de Faucon, my grandfather being French, but he called himself Falcon and I took my mother's name.'

'Had you no other relatives?'

'My mother had a twin brother somewhere, but we've not heard of him in years. Why, you're shivering, love! We'll find more blankets for you.'

She was cold to the marrow, Godwin de Faucon had talked briefly of his sister and of the castle of Marie Regina. there couldn't possibly be two places of the same name in Kent.

In a small voice she said, 'Did you — did you ever have a seal, a silver claw?'

'I believe I did. The duke, my father, gave it to me once. His first wife, the Duchess Blanche, had had two of them made. I don't know what happened to the one I was given. I fear I'm sometimes careless with my possessions.'

'And the other?'

'The other seal? My mother had it.'

'And gave it to me,' Diana thought. 'She put it in my hands and sent me down to the river to hide with Becky from the peasants. It's coming back to me now; all these years a dream has been a memory and I was too close to the picture to be able to see it clearly.

'How did you know about the seal?' Maudelyn asked, blowing out the candle and clambering into the bed beside her.

'Someone mentioned it,' she said vaguely.

Another memory was pushing its way to the surface of her mind.

Master Ralph Aston had told her of the great wrong Godwin de Faucon had done to him when he had seduced his sweetheart. Godwin had deserted the maid, and his sister had fled with her, sending back word that the girl had died of a miscarriage. But if the child had lived, if the child had been a girl and lived?

'You're still shivering,' Maudelyn said, and he put his arms about her, holding her close in the darkness.

Her thoughts ran on.

'If Godwin de Faucon is my father then I was spared from a dreadful sin, and there was some use then in my parents' deaths. It's a hard truth but truth *is* hard. In the end we all come to our rightful places. And that means that Maudelyn is my cousin. 'Tis no wonder that I was drawn to him in the beginning.'

Aloud she said, 'I will be a good wife to you, Maudelyn. You'll not regret settling down with me.'

The next morning, as soon as she had steadied herself after the usual bout of sickness and nausea, they set off on the final stage of their journey. There was much that Diana could have talked about now to Maudelyn, but she kept silent. He had never mentioned a child called Diana, but then he had been reared by his father and might not be aware of what had happened. She would wait until she had met Gida Falcon, and then make up her mind what to do.

'The monastery is just ahead of us,' Maudelyn said, pointing through the rain, 'I remember my mother telling me long ago when she was a girl, the Abbot was burned for heresy. They're all good churchmen there now!'

They rode past the grey crowned tor over a wooden bridge towards wooded banks beyond. The landscape was blurred and softened by the falling rain and the whole scene had a remote, dreamlike quality.

Diana gazed round with almost painful intensity, desperately trying to remember, to shrink down into the small child again. A small child who cried for Becky and held onto a silver claw seal. She was not certain if she could really recall anything or was only imagining that she could remember.

'The castle is about three miles further on,' Maudelyn said. 'All this land is church property but they lease it out.'

'It's been a bad harvest.' She shielded her eyes to gaze at the sodden pastures.

'Too much rain, and a hard winter to follow if the luck runs badly,' he agreed.

'Will you mind very much spending the winter here?' she asked anxiously.

'Better then being camped in the Welsh

267

mountains without my wife to warm my pallet,' he said.

He spoke as if he were used to her being his wife, as if the idea of it had settled in his mind and pleased him.

They reached open gates that sagged a little on their hinges and rode up an avenue of trees to the high towered building ahead. It was more like a fort than a castle, she thought, staring up at it. The postern gate was open and, as they rode into the courtyard, a man with a hooded smock on put his head out of the stable door and said loudly, 'Mistress Falcon's from home.'

'I am Maudelyn Falcon and this is my wife.' Maudelyn swung himself to the ground and lifted Diana down.

'Lord, but we weren't told there'd been a wedding!' the man exclaimed. 'I'm Simon, Mistress Falcon's man of all work.'

'See to the horses then, Simon. Where is my lady mother?' Maudelyn asked.

'Ridden away, but she said she'd be back before winter came. Bess is in the kitchen and she'll get you something to eat.'

'In here, love.' Maudelyn took Diana's arm, guiding her across the cobbles to the main door.

It opened into a high-raftered hall with a central hearth on which a cheerful fire burned. A staircase curved out of the hall and from an open door at the back came the sound of singing which broke off abruptly as a maidservant hurried out.

'Are you Bess?' Maudelyn enquired.

'Yes, master.' The woman bobbed a curtsey. 'Alison and I work in the kitchens here. You must be — '

'Maudelyn Falcon. Simon tells me that my lady mother is not at home.'

'No, sir. She went visiting about a month since, but we'll see her back very soon, I'm certain. She never goes away from home as a rule.'

'Is there a room prepared?'

'There's the tower room, above the one where the mistress sleeps. I can air some linen.'

'Get us something to eat first.' He put his arm about Diana and led her to the stairs.

They twisted up past a handsome bed-chamber into another apartment, furnished also with bed, chairs and a wardrobe. Warm hued tapestries hung against the stone walls and arrow slit windows looked out over the fields and trees to the narrow ribbon of river beyond.

'I'd slept here when Petrella had her babe,' Maudelyn said, and stopped, frowning as if he were not sure why he had made the statement.

'Petrella?'

'A girl who came with us from London,' he said slowly. 'She had a babe and died of it. I don't know what happened to the babe because my lady mother took me up to Kenilworth, to my father's estate. Odd, but I hadn't thought about that for years.'

'Do you remember the name of the babe?' Diana asked in a small voice.

Maudelyn considered for a moment, then shook his head.

'It's gone,' he said. 'I can't think what made me speak of it.'

'The babe's name was Diana,' she told him. 'She was the daughter of your uncle, of Godwin de Faucon, his natural daughter, but he never knew she had been born at all. Your own mother reared the babe and then the peasants came and so Aunt Gida sent her to hide in the woods down by the river with Becky and — there was Becky's father too, but I forget his name. He and Becky were Jews, and the peasants killed them for it, and snatched away the child. They took her with them on their march to London, but she ran away from them in the confusion — '

'And was reared by some people called Maundy. Is that what you're saying to me?'

'We are cousins,' she said simply. 'It has taken me many years to work it out. My aunt gave me a seal, a silver claw like the one you had, but, like you, I lost my seal too.'

'My cousin and now my wife? And you have only just discovered it?'

She nodded, her anxious eyes on his face.

'You will want to find your father,' he said. 'We have not heard from him in years.'

'No!' she said sharply. 'Your mother must have had a good reason for concealing the birth. Leave it as it is.'

Not even to Maudelyn could she speak of Ralph Aston's or her parents' deaths. Better to keep silent and pray that he would never return to Marie Regina.

'My mother has not mentioned you in all these years,' he said. 'To keep her anxiety and grief to herself in such a fashion — I told you she was a remarkable woman!'

'You are not angry are you, at my not having told you before? I was not sure how to frame it, but then you began to remember yourself.'

'Not much,' he said. 'I was more interested in climbing trees and playing at archers at that age than in girl babies. And then I was taken to my father and afterwards saw my mother very seldom. She wanted

271

me to have the advantage of a knightly education.'

'And we met at last, without knowing it, in the church,' she said softly.

'There is a pattern in it,' said Maudelyn.

'And one not ended. Your child will be born in March.'

'We will name him John, after my father,' he decided.

'It might be a girl,' she objected.

'No, it will be a boy,' he said with such certainty that she wanted to laugh.

'And will you stay here with me?' She looked round, her eyes measuring the chamber. 'You are used to riding free up and down the land, and you've been on campaign with the king. Won't you find it dull in this quiet place?'

'I shall learn to be a farmer,' he assured her. 'I will set my mind on being lord of the manor, and learn how to increase my profits even after a wet summer. There must be other neighbours apart from the monks. We will give hunting parties and balls and marry our sons to the prettiest damsels in Kent.'

His green eyes were sparkling, his voice lively. Looking at him, Diana felt much older and wiser than her years. She loved Maudelyn, but she could see that there was something cool and elusive in his nature and that it would never be pinned down in matrimony. He was basically self-absorbed, seeing himself now in a new role as lord of the manor. He had not troubled to enquire into the details of her life with the Maundys or into their deaths or the reason for her entering the convent. She had the uncomfortable suspicion that if she were to vanish from sight for another eight years he would realise vaguely that something was missing in his life, and greet her without question if she returned. It would be hard to hold him, but then the duke had warned her about that many years before.

'There is someone riding into the courtyard,' he said, interrupting his own narrative to peer down into the rainswept enclosure. 'Lord, but I swear it's my lady mother!'

Diana was on her feet, out of the room, and down the twisting stairs almost before the words were out of his mouth. She ran across the hall and tugged open the heavy door, blinking up at the cloaked and hooded figure.

Simon came from the stable to help the newcomer to dismount, and the woman came towards Diana, pushing her sodden hood back from her greying hair. Her thin face was alight with joy but her voice was hoarsely scolding as she held out a silver claw seal.

'You must learn to take better care of your things now that you are come home again,' she said.

Part Three

15

1410

'Something is troubling you,' Gida said, glancing at her silent niece.

'Is it so obvious?' Diana looked up from the tunic she was mending and smiled at the older woman.

'I know your moods,' Gida said. 'You have been smiling too brightly and speaking too little for weeks. What troubles you?'

'Maudelyn is going back to Court,' Diana said abruptly.

'He mentioned it to me. Will you go with him?'

'I'll not leave the children, and I'll not drag them into the smoke of the city,' Diana said.

'Is it so terrible that he should want to visit the Court again?' Gida asked gently. 'Gentlemen do sometimes spend time away from their homes, you know, and Maudelyn has been here for the past seven years.'

'Is that so dreadful?' Diana asked with a flash of indignation. 'This is a beautiful place and we are happy together.'

'My dear, you have made him a splendid wife,' Gida said warmly. 'You mustn't begin to imagine that he is discontented with you because he wishes to enter the wider world again for a few short months.'

'And if he doesn't return?'

'Do you fear he will not?' Gida looked at the younger woman shrewdly. 'Is that what troubles you?'

'Maudelyn is restless. He hides it from me, but I can sense it in him. If he goes back to Court he may discover after all that he cannot endure a rural life any longer.'

'You never knew my father, did you?' Gida said softly. 'Pierre de Faucon, taken prisoner at Neville's Cross and sent here, to Marie Regina, to await his ransom. He never went back to his old home. He stayed here and married my mother, and after he had married her he went away again. We spent a little time together as a family in London and then he went away into Flanders or Provence — I forget where. By the time he returned my mother had died of the plague. She had loved my father very much but she never spoke a word of complaint to him when he left her.'

'Then she ought to have done,' Diana said bluntly.

'I used to think that when I was a child,'

Gida said, 'but my mother was wiser. She knew there was a restlessness in my father and that she could only hold him by setting him free. Let Maudelyn go to Court now and he'll come back. There is great restlessness in him too, but you have had him close at home for seven years. Now you must wave him goodbye and await his return.'

'You make it sound so easy,' Diana said resentfully.

'It is the hardest thing in the world,' Gida told her. 'It is also the only thing to do. We women have great influence, you know, which we may use for good or evil.'

'Queen Joanna said something like that to me once,' Diana mused.

'About the power of women?'

'And how one day they would rise and use their ancient power.'

'I've heard that Joanna of Navarre is whispered by some to be a heretic, by others a witch,' Gida said in a casual tone. 'What was your opinion of her?'

'That she was strange but more unhappy than evil,' Diana said slowly.

Gida folded away her own work and asked, 'Where are the children?'

'The boys went riding with Maudelyn. He was going to show them how to set snares.'

'And Alice and Alfreda?'

'Are in the orchard with Bess.'

'Then there is nothing to prevent you and me from taking a ride over to the monastery,' Gida said.

'It will be dark before we return.'

'We'll leave word with Simon,' Gida said. 'Go tell him to saddle up the horses and tell him too that Bess is not to wait supper if we are a little late.'

Diana had little desire to go riding in her present mood, but Gida was in one of her spells of firm obstinacy when argument would have been useless.

She went through to the stables, gave the message to Simon, and then lingered for a few minutes at the gate to watch the distant figures of the children as they played in and out of the apple trees. From this distance in their red kirtles and blue sashes they looked no bigger than dolls. Alice at three was the prettier and more strong willed of the pair, her yellow curls tumbling about her rosy face, her shrill little voice demanding. Alfreda was gentler, her hair spiky and of a dark red colour that reminded Diana of beech leaves. She was not yet two and still unsteady on her feet, but staggered about in pursuit of the ball, never complaining when the more energetic Alice reached it first. Diana would never have admitted it to anybody, but she loved Alfreda more than her other children. The boys, John and William, were sturdy editions of their father with the same lank fair hair and narrow green eyes. In a year or two they would be sent as pages into some rich lord's household, but for the time being they stayed close to their father, imitating everything he did in a manner that was both endearing and irritating.

'Come along, do,' Gida said from behind her, 'or it will be dark before we get there.'

'I can't think why we're going,' Diana grumbled, mounting unwillingly. 'The community will all be at Benediction.'

'Good. Then we shall be unobserved,' Gida said calmly, mounting almost as nimbly as the younger woman. Although she was approaching sixty her health was excellent, her digestion sound, and her faculties unimpaired. She gave her niece a look of warm approval. Diana was lovelier than she had ever been, her hair more ripely golden, her figure more rounded, her eyes marked only by faint laughter lines.

'It's my belief that Maudelyn will be back from Court before winter sets in,' she said, and trotted briskly through the gates.

In early June the land was all green and gold and white blossom under a canopy of blue sky. Dotted about the landscape were a few wattle and daub structures where the local peasants lived, but between the monastery and the high towered castle there were no buildings. Only trees and the winding river marked the scene and over all brooded a tranquillity that seemed to impart an added lustre to the beauty of leaf and petal.

'Nature shows us the brightness of the skirts of the Goddess,' Gida said as they came within sight of the river.

'The Goddess?' Diana's voice was raised in surprise.

'You will have heard the queen speak of the Goddess, if the queen is what I take her to be,' Gida said. 'We'll dismount here and tether the horses among the trees. No sense in telling the whole world what we're doing.'

'I thought we were going to the monastery,' Diana objected, following the other down the bridle path.

'In good time. Learn to be less impatient,' Gida said.

Diana held her peace, threading her way between the trees to the river's edge where in a small glade a hut stood, it's walls covered in creeper.

'My mother lived here before her marriage, and her mother before her,' Gida said.

'You told me,' Diana said patiently.

'And may tell you again. I'm at the age when I'm permitted to repeat myself,' Gida said, 'but what I'm about to tell you I've not told you before. Oh, if you hadn't been stolen away I would have passed on the knowledge to you long ago, but there! Now it's seven years since your return and I'm not getting any younger.'

'Knowledge? What knowledge?'

'The Ancient Wisdom,' said Gida, 'is so old that one cannot tell when it was first entrusted to mankind. All we do know is that it cannot be given to all because the power such knowledge bestows can be used for good or evil purpose. It is handed down among those who follow the ancient ways, and those ways are called heresy and witchcraft by those who cannot understand.'

'There was an Abbot burned once from the monastery here,' Diana said.

'My mother received her training from him.' Gida said, 'and now I must pass it on to you, as you yourself will pass it on one day. But you must guard your knowledge carefully.'

'The queen spoke of the power of the Goddess,' Diana said. 'Who is the Goddess?'

'She is in all women,' Gida said, 'and her power is boundless. You will learn much from the Goddess if you listen to your heart. Women weave the pattern of the world, child, and the pattern has the rhythm of the seasons in it and the sound of the tides rushing up to meet the moon.'

'The queen celebrated Midsummer, but only with her close attendants and we were bidden not to speak of it.'

'Solstice,' Gida nodded. 'Come with me now. We cross the bridge and climb the tor on foot. I have something to show you.'

Diana followed again, crossing the wooden bridge and climbing up the winding path to the high walls that surrounded the cloisters and garden of the monastery. The Brethren were at prayer at this hour and the faint sound of chanting voices stirred the quiet air.

'This way,' Gida said. Her voice was low but there was a suppressed excitement in her manner. Diana noticed that she cast a swift look around before she took a key from within her cloak and inserted it in the lock of a drably painted door.

'It was locked when the old Abbot was burned,' she said. 'I doubt if any of the present monks dream of its existence. Come!'

The door swung open into a narrow, rocky passage twisting into darkness. Gida took lamp and tinder box from a ledge at the side and kindled the wick. Then she stepped within, motioning to Diana to close the door behind her.

'This small cave was where the one about to be initiated into the Ancient Wisdom waited,' she said, holding the lamp high to show a mossgrown cavern in which water trickled down to a deep pool. 'There are hidden air shafts all through these caves, they must be thousands of years old, and now I am the only one left who comes here.'

'For what purpose?'

'To keep the lamp flickering for a little while until the heavy hand of the official Church snuffs it out,' Gida said.

The passage widened into an antechamber and three rock hewn steps led to a narrow portal. For a moment the younger woman hesitated. Row after row of invisible presences seemed to crowd in upon her. Then she followed her aunt up the stairs and through the arched entrance.

A vast hall, with a smaller chamber beyond, curved about her, its rock walls smooth. In the centre below the arched roof an altar of black stone reared. Against each wall was set an immense carved chair of the same black stone, and behind each chair, painted on the wall, a winged figure towered up into shadow. 'The Archangels of the Quarters,' Gida said. 'Raphael for healing, Michael for protection,

Gabriel for news from heaven, Uriel for the instincts of earth. Make them your friends, for we balance their elements in our own natures.'

'Were ceremonies held here?' Diana whispered.

'By those Templar Knights who fled the persecution of the Church and lived here as monks, keeping faith with the Ancient Mysteries. Many died for it,' Gida said.

'The Abbot?'

'And many others too,' Gida told her. 'Good, brave men who died for their beliefs having confessed, under torture, to abominations they never committed.'

'But not the Abbot?'

'The Abbot was never questioned, and he went silent to the fire,' Gida said proudly. 'Now it's for you and me to carry on the traditions and pass them on to those who will use the knowledge wisely.'

'It must have been wonderful,' Diana said wistfully, 'to have been here when the great ceremonies took place. There would have been lights, I suppose?'

'And great incense burners,' Gida nodded. 'There was a golden cross once above the altar and jewelled cups, swords, wands. They were all taken away when the Abbot was arrested, and the door was locked. I come here when I can, at Solstice and Equinox, and invoke the ancient ones who rule the watch-towers of the world.'

'And you will teach me these things?'

'Little by little,' Gida promised. 'I know only what I myself have been told, and much you will have to glean for yourself. Does it sound a formidable task?'

'An adventure,' Diana said, 'but I'd not want to be called a heretic.'

'Those who are called heretic today are called genius tomorrow,' Gida said. 'But we don't speak of such matters in public, for that would be to risk — more than we should ever be expected to give.'

'It will be Midsummer soon,' Diana said.

'We will come here on that night,' Gida said. 'You and I will come here when the moon is full and we will eat honey cake and drink wine in honour of the Goddess, and we will sing the ancient moon song that my mother once sang to me. And you will gain strength from the Goddess, the strength to make Maudelyn go back to Court as he wishes and the strength to lure him back again before winter comes.'

'Yes.' Diana spoke gently, her gaze still circling the hall.

There was a reality here, a purity of line and will that had nothing to do with Queen

Joanna's perfumed parties. Yet she knew that the queen too worshipped the Goddess in her own way, and nobody could truly judge the path on which the feet of another were set.

They walked back in silence and Gida carefully blew out the lamp and locked the door behind them again.

Through the wide archway they could see the quiet garden, its beds of vegetables edged with sweet smelling herbs, fruit bushes ranged along the wall. Two of the laybrothers, habits flapping about their ankles, emerged from the chapel and walked towards them.

Gida raised her hand in greeting and called to them. 'Good-morrow. Is Service over?'

'I fear you have missed it,' one of the monks said, flapping towards them. 'Did you come to see the Abbot, Mistress Falcon?'

'Not particularly. Mistress Diana and I are enjoying the sunset.'

'It is very beautiful,' the monk said. 'There are times when I'm tempted to waste a few minutes of my labour and just gaze at the beauty of it. 'Tis only the thought of the penance to follow that stops me.'

He smiled and padded back to his companion.

'They have their place in the pattern too,' Gida said. 'Come, we must start back. It will be dusk soon.'

'You surely don't fear the dark!' Diana exclaimed.

'No, but 'tis dark of the moon,' Gida said, ' 'tis a good plan to be safe indoors when the moon is dark, for at that time the name of the Goddess is Hecate, she who guards the threshold of the dreaming mind.'

'I have much to learn,' Diana said humbly.

'Oh, you will learn so quickly that you will not remember soon what it was like to open the first door,' Gida said affectionately.

'There's Maudelyn and the boys!' Diana said, beginning to hurry down the path.

Gida followed more slowly. There were times when she wished to be alone, for much as she loved the children their boisterousness sometimes wearied her.

'Have you been to church?' Maudelyn swung himself to the ground and kissed Diana on the cheek.

'Just up to the cloister,' she said vaguely. 'It's a beautiful evening.'

'We snared a coney!' six year old John called. 'We're going to get Bess to skin it and cook it with some onions for supper.'

'You're a clever lad!' she approved.

'Ride on ahead then and tell her to get it started,' Maudelyn ordered. 'Where's your horse, Diana? Surely you and my lady mother didn't walk all the way here!'

'Of course not. They're tethered in the wood.' She hurried ahead of him across the bridge and down the bridle path. Gida had paused on her way down the path and now waved Maudelyn to go on.

He followed his wife, his eyes on her back. Her blue cloak with its hood suited her colouring. She had grown a little plumper in recent months and that suited her too. His eyes kindled as he remembered how soft and yielding she had been the previous night. She was a lovely and loving wife and he was a fortunate man. He sighed, quickening his step a little.

'It's a funny thing,' Diana said, turning to face him as they reached the river bank, 'but when I was younger, before I knew my history, I had nightmares about this place. It is still the same place but I have no nightmares about it now.'

'Or about anything else, I hope.'

'You have made me so very happy!' she cried impulsively. 'I believe we were meant to marry, meant to settle down together.'

'Yes. To settle down,' he repeated.

There was a faint constraint in his smile. Diana saw it and her own smile wavered a little.

'John is becoming quite a hunter,' Maudelyn said. 'William needs more confidence, I fear, but he is little yet. I think he will be more of the scholar.'

'I have been thinking,' she said, lifting her chin, 'of what we were talking about yesterday, of your returning to Court for a while.'

'It was no more than a whim,' he said.

'I think you ought to go,' she said gravely. 'After all it must be many years since you met any of your former acquaintances.'

'I never made close friends,' he said.

'But you were always so busy,' she said excusingly, 'that you had no time for friends. Now that you are settled then there's no reason why you shouldn't visit the Court again.'

'Will you ride with me? That would please me.'

'It would please me too,' she said lightly, 'but the children are too little to be left.'

'My lady mother — '

'Is nearly sixty and the boys weary her. And Bess cannot bear to refuse Alice anything at all, so that the child is becoming wilful and self indulged. No, my love, in a year or two I'll ride with you to Court and we will have a wonderful time, but for now I believe it would do you a great deal of good.'

'And the estate — ?'

'That will be here when you return,' she

said cheerfully. 'You are not indispensable, you know! The land was worked for years before you came, and your lady mother and I will see to the household.'

'It would only be for a month or two,' he said.

'You'll be back when the harvest is gathered in,' she said.

'Bless you!' He put his arms around her and kissed her heartily. 'I will miss you terribly. No woman at Court will ever compare with you for beauty and an understanding heart.'

'I shall take it ill if you stay long enough with any Court lady to begin to make any comparisons at all!' she joked.

'I will keep my rosary in my hands and I will tell every female I meet that I have taken a vow of chastity for the summer!' he retorted.

'Your lady mother is here.' Diana waved to the small figure descending the path.

'And quite capable of mounting myself,' Gida said crisply. 'What were you both laughing about just now?'

'I have decided to send Maudelyn to Court,' Diana said, brightly smiling. 'It will do him good to see other folk apart from ourselves.'

'And it will do us good to be able to

sweeten the house without having a man march in and out with mud on his boots,' Gida said. 'Oh, we shall manage very well without you for a time. Come, we'll catch up the children!'

She rode ahead of them, reaching out to touch Diana's hand in passing.

'You're sure you don't mind my going?' Maudelyn asked, a sudden doubt in his face.

'I shall be very glad not to have you under my feet,' she said.

'I'll bring you all gifts from London,' he promised. 'Daggers for the boys, dolls for the girls, a new kirtle for my lady mother, and for you — for you a betrothal ring!'

'I never liked them,' she said quickly.

'Nonsense! After seven years of wedlock it should be a gift for which you've been nagging me,' he said roundly. 'I fear you don't demand enough from me, my dear.'

'I have everything I need,' she said simply.

'I'll bring you something all the same,' he promised.

There was no doubt that he loved her. There was equally no doubt that he would be delighted to be free of her for a few months. Diana felt immeasurably older and wiser as they rode home.

The girls were still up, though it was past

their bedtime. Maudelyn took Alice on his knee, his face tender, for the spirited little girl was his favourite. Alfreda, her thumb in her mouth, leaned back comfortably against Gida's arm. The boys were in the kitchen, giving Bess much unwanted advice about the stew.

Diana glanced about the raftered hall with its cheerful fire and wished passionately they could all stay warm and safe for ever, but Maudelyn was going to Court and the moon was dark.

16

'It really is good to see you again after so long a time!' Prince Henry clasped Maudelyn's hands warmly.

'I have not yet been received in audience,' Maudelyn said. 'A week at Westminster and no greeting from the king! A few more days and I shall begin to fear I have become invisible!'

'My father is in one of his private moods,' the prince grimaced. 'He has periods when he sits alone in his apartments, seeing nobody, speaking to nobody.'

'Cannot the queen help?'

'My stepmother?' The young man's handsome face darkened and he lowered his voice. 'My stepmother is an enchantress. No! Don't smile for I speak literal truth. Oh, she goes to Mass and she tells her beads and confesses her sins, but she keeps the old ways too. I know it but I cannot prove it. The king will hear nothing against her.'

'She is a comely woman.' Maudelyn glanced down the great hall with its chattering throng of nobles to where Joanna sat on her dais, purple robes spread about her.

'And the Devil, they say, is beautiful,' the prince muttered. 'I remember my own mother too well to be deceived by this Joanna.'

Maudelyn was silent, sensing that it would be useless to try to alter the other's opinion. Hal, for all his roistering reputation, was narrowly Christian, and in his eyes the woodland gods were all demons and the Great Goddess a perpetual Hecate.

'Tell me about the Welsh campaign,' he invited instead, and Hal launched at once into an account of the deep valleys and high hills, the freezing winds that blew down from the heights, the tribesmen in their cloaks and breeches.

'But you should have been with us,' he said. 'You have buried yourself in the country these many years.'

'I'm a married man now, with four younglings,' Maudelyn reminded him.

'And I have a taste for all wenches,' the prince grinned, 'which is why I refuse to accept any of the foreign princesses my royal father has been pushing at me. When I wed I will remain faithful and I'm not of age for that yet.'

'You are also fond of campaigning,' Maudelyn commented.

'I like to keep busy,' the prince said

vaguely. 'There is trouble in Burgundy now, and it would please me to raise a small expedition to investigate the matter. The Council will grant me the money, I'm certain.'

'When do you leave?'

'Within the month, but we'll be home again before winter. It may all come to nothing, but it's better than wasting my time here. Will you come with me, or do you hold my father's opinion that I am still a schoolboy to be scolded when I do anything on my own account?'

'Home before winter?'

'With largesse,' the prince tempted.

'Then I'll join you,' Maudelyn decided.

'If your wife gives her consent?' Hal gave him a mischievous look.

'My wife never questions what I do,' Maudelyn said stiffly, but his mind ran on, completing the sentence, 'as long as you do it in her company.'

Aloud he said, a trifle heartily, 'We'll talk later, sir. I have been housebound for so long that I forget my manners and neglect to greet old friends.'

The prince nodded, clapping him on the shoulder before he moved away.

To go to Burgundy was a tempting idea. He had not been out of England for years and though he had believed himself to be content, he realised now that he had been confined. A loving and pleasant confinement, but a confinement all the same. And Diana would have no objections. In fact it would be possible to leave and come back again without her realising he had even sailed.

The queen was beckoning to him. He went towards her, bowing, his eyes admiringly on her warmly welcoming smile and jewel threaded hair.

'Your Grace.' He kissed her plump hand and took the stool she indicated.

'We have not had the opportunity of talking to you since you came to Court,' she said. 'So many years since we have seen you, and we are all older.'

'Your Grace does not look it,' he said gallantly, but it was not quite true. Her eyes were lost in a network of fine lines and there was a disappointed droop to her mouth. Her skin was too heavily painted, he thought, for a woman who was completely happy.

'I have had troubles — ' she said slowly.

'I am sorry to hear it,' He looked a question and after a moment she rose, waving her attendants aside, leaning on his arm as she made her way through a side entrance into a long, painted corridor that led to a small, enclosed courtyard.

'We can talk more freely here,' Joanna said. 'There are so many people here to listen to what one says and to twist the meaning around. I tell you that there are people at Court who would do anything to bring grief upon me.'

'You speak of the prince,' Maudelyn said.

'Who is a friend of yours?' She shot him one of her keen, shrewed glances.

'My nephew in blood,' Maudelyn agreed, 'but he was only a boy when I left Court.'

'A boy devoted to the memory of two people,' Joanna said. 'His uncle, king Richard, whose place his father usurped, and his mother, Mary de Bohun, whose place I usurped. We are both guilty in Hal's eyes, but he is fond of his father so I am the one upon whom he fixes his blame.'

'Cannot the king speak on your behalf?' Maudelyn asked.

'The king is not well,' she said, a faint sharpness in her voice. 'He must not be troubled!'

'What ails His Grace?'

'It is given out that he has attacks of the ague, which is true and most distressing they are for him,' she said.

'Given out?' He frowned and spoke with as much authority as he dare.

'You and the king shared the same father,'

Joanna said. They had reached the courtyard but she passed through its gate into the wooded glade beyond as if she feared eavesdroppers.

'John of Gaunt,' he nodded.

'And you are loyal to Henry? You have no political ambition?'

'If I had any political ambition,' he said wryly, 'I'd not have spent so many years buried in the country.'

'The king suffers from a disease,' Joanna said, lowering her voice still further and glancing around. 'It has not yet taken hold of him completely. There are long periods when he is better, so much better there is no trace of the sickness.'

'What do the doctors say?' he queried.

'They say that the periods of good health will grow fewer and last a shorter time,' she said. 'And the ravages of the disease will become apparent.'

'What is the disease?' he asked.

'The king is a leper,' she said flatly.

'A leper!' He breathed the word in horror.

'It does not show itself yet save in a deadening of the fingers and a rigidity of the muscles of the face,' Joanna said. 'I have some skill with herbs and remedies, but I fear that in a year or two he will be beyond my help. And the prince is an ambitious man. If he ever guessed the true nature of his father's illness then he would certainly force abdication upon him and seize the crown.'

'If the king is so ill,' Maudelyn ventured, 'Might it not be better for him to retire from public life. Prince Hal is an intelligent man, popular with the people.'

'And eager for power,' she nodded. 'Oh, I have no doubt he'll make an excellent monarch when the time comes, but that time is not yet. I tell you, Master Falcon, it is not solely on the king's account that I keep this knowledge to myself. The prince detests me. Can you imagine how soon I might be — removed, if the king abdicated?'

'The prince is honourable and would not stoop to murder,' Maudelyn defended.

'Not murder.' her eyes were wide and strained as if she gazed into the future. 'The prince is a devout Churchman for all his wild ways. He has no sympathy with ancient belief, no real love for the Goddess even though he does spend so much time with the wenches. I am already distrusted by the clergy, for there are always rumours. I have no wish to be accused of heresy and locked up for the rest of my life.'

'Would it come to that?'

'It's likely, when the king is rendered

powerless, so I delay it for as long as I can,' she said sombrely.

'Then I will say nothing,' he said gravely. 'The prince goes to Burgundy soon.'

'To play at soldiers,' she said with a little flash of spite. 'Well, it will amuse him, I've no doubt. And will you go with him?'

'Until the end of the summer,' he nodded. 'I am out of the habit of travelling.'

'But have lived a faithful husband,' she observed. 'Your wife is well, I hope? She was a maid ripe for marriage when I first saw her. You will convey my greetings to her when you see her again?'

'Of course, madam.' He bowed, his hand clasping hers for a moment.

'You must excuse me now,' Joanna said, her glance flickering to two of her ladies who were strolling towards her, their bright skirts whispering across the grass. She gave a slight shake of the head at him as if to remind him of his pledge of secrecy, and moved away, her voice raised in cheerfulness.

'Ladies, have you no escorts to enliven your walk? Come, we'll go indoors or would you prefer to come down to the butts with me? We will persuade some of the gentlemen away from their sport.'

They walked away together, the queen

moving with plump grace between the more slender, younger women. Gazing after them Maudelyn was reminded of Diana. She too had put on a little weight in recent years. Her breasts were fuller, her hips more rounded. It occurred to him that she had begun to glow rather than sparkle. There was sadness in the thought, as if something fresh and delicate were beginning to fade.

He walked back slowly, aware of the restlessness in him that had not been quenched by the quietness of the years at Marie Regina. He was, he supposed, near middleaged but he felt like a young man. There was not an ounce of spare flesh on his lean frame and no grey in his lank blond hair.

'You are sad, sir.'

The voice made him jump for it seemed to come out of nowhere. Then he saw that a young woman had emerged from the courtyard and was looking at him, her head on one side.

'Forgive me, but I didn't see you, mistress,' he apologised.

He could not see her clearly now, for her face was in shadow and further shaded by coils of brown hair that blended with the silvery-brown dress she wore. Their shapes were pulled out long and thin across the grass and behind the high wall the sky was tinged with red.

'I watched you with Her Grace,' the girl said.

'And heard?' He reached out to grip her arm. 'Did you hear?'

'No, sir.' She stood calmly, not trying to break free. 'You were too far away and spoke too low for anyone to hear.'

'Are you one of Her Grace's ladies?' He bent, trying to see her face more clearly. It was a narrow face, the bones delicate, the skin milky white, the lips full and inviting.

'I am Louise,' she said. 'Nothing else about me is important.'

'My name is Maudelyn,' he began, but she put up a long, slim hand, her eyes glinting between sooty lashes, her voice teasing.

'No more. We are both visitors to Court. Let us meet on that level while we are here.'

'Very well.' He released his grasp and stepped back a pace. 'Do I take it that you expect us to meet?'

'Her Grace gives a private supper later tonight in her apartments,' Louise said. 'Will you come?'

'So she still gives these private suppers?' Maudelyn whistled softly. Remembering other occasions when the queen had invited young men and women to dance and love under her enigmatic gaze.

'Now and then, when the king is indisposed, when Prince Hal treats her without respect. She gives supper parties then.'

'I am wed,' he said foolishly.

'No matter,' she said indifferently. 'Come if you wish, or not — as the mood takes you. I am joining the others now.'

She had turned and was speeding across the grass, her long hair floating behind her in the gathering dusk. He stared after her, watching until she was lost to sight amid the trees.

The prince, with a group of his attendants, left shortly after supper. It was his custom to roister about the town as several of the staider members of the Court had already confided to Maudelyn. The prince was a devout Christian, but he was happily sowing his wild oats.

'And I sowed mine,' Maudelyn thought. 'One cannot turn back. I am married now, with four children, and a wife who loves me. Lord! I am nearer forty than twenty, and my green days are past.'

But the young woman who had spoken to him at the courtyard gate lingered in his mind. It was not that he loved or desired her, but there was something mysterious and provocative in the thought of her. He loved Diana but she had lost her first sharp sweetness, and she would be there when he returned, warm and wise and unquestioning, like a comfortable habit that rounded his existence.

The queen's apartments were guarded as usual when he reached them, but before he could give his name the girl slipped her hand into his, nodded reassuringly at the halberdier, and drew Maudelyn into the dim and scented chamber. He felt absurdly pleased that she had waited for him, but her low voice mocked as she led him towards the table where the wine and honeycakes were spread.

'So you are not a coward, sir? You are so late that I began to wonder.'

'I too wondered,' he said.

'About me?'

'About the wisdom of coming tonight. I am wed.'

'Aye, you told me, but I'd have known without,' she said. 'You wear your wedded state like a halter.'

'I am happily married,' he said, and despised the primness of his voice.

'Of course you are,' she said softly. 'That is why it is in your power to give pleasure to other women. Come, you'd not practise selfishness, would you?'

'Some call it faithfulness,' he chided, and she laughed, her teeth white and sharp between her full lips.

'Drink some of the wine and let us join the dance,' she said. 'We must honour the Goddess.'

'Who did not invite me.' He glanced towards the centre of the room where the queen stood, leaning against a pillar, her face hidden beneath its mask of paint, her hair plaited with ropes of pearl and crystal.

'She knows that you were going to come,' Louise said.

'How could she, when I didn't know it myself?'

In answer she tapped the side of her nose and gave him a slanting female glance. Gida and Diana gave him the same look sometimes, as if all women were bound in a conspiracy.

'Dance with me,' he said impatiently.

'Of course,' She came into his arms like silk, winding herself around him with a gentle persistence. A scent of musk rose from her skin and hair, exciting his senses, and he drew her closer, and saw beyond her the queen smiling at them both.

'Must we dance in the circle?' he asked Louise softly. 'Cannot we slip away now?'

'To the galleries?' She glanced towards the narrow staircase, but he shook his head.

'I have been lodged in a separate room,' he told her.

'The queen will not be pleased. She likes to watch.'

'There are plenty here to satisfy her taste,' he argued. 'Will you come?'

'If you wish,' she said, docile as a kitten. He moved with her towards the door, hoping the queen would not notice him, but Joanna had turned aside to take a sugar plum from a dish held by one of the pages.

'Why do you want to take me to your room?' Louise asked.

'I like my love-making to be private,' he said briefly.

He couldn't begin to explain, even to himself, why he had no wish to make love to her on the gallery. It had something to do with his sense of the fitness of things. Diana and he had first coupled at one of the queen's private entertainments, and that episode was held like a jewel in his memory. It was not to be tarnished by this brief episode that had in it no more than the snatching at a boyhood that was gone.

Not quite gone, he thought, dismissing Diana from his mind as this younger woman pressed against him, her eyes modestly lowered, the tops of her breasts pouting over the bodice of her silvery brown dress.

'You are like a moth,' he said.

'A moth? That's a pretty conceit,' she murmured and laughed on a chime of bells.

The chamber where he was lodged was small but, as most gentlemen were expected to share a bed, he considered himself unusually fortunate. He bolted the door and turned to attend to the candles.

'This is a very private place,' she said thoughtfully, and laughed on a higher note as if she were gripped by excitement.

'Tell me something of yourself,' he began, but she shook her head, murmuring, 'Later. Help me with my gown now.'

His fingers shook a little as he undid the laces. Beneath the gown she wore a plain white shift and for a moment, as she stood there, she looked like a very sweet, very obedient child. Then in one swift, fluid gesture she let the white garment crumple about her feet and she was no longer a child but a young Venus who had existed since the beginning of time. She was all the maids he had loved in his bachelor days, all the women he had denied himself in the years of his marriage; and in a curious way she was Diana herself before domestic life had robbed her of her mystery.

That much he realised and then he was conscious only of her hair, her perfume, the hunger in his loins, and the faint radiance of the candle as he bore her to the bed.

He had not expected her to be virgin and she was not, but neither had he expected her frantic response as if she were drowning and trying to pull him down with her, the breath harsh in her throat, her nails scoring his back.

'Tell me now about yourself,' she said at last, as he rolled away from her, fumbling for a piece of the blanket to wipe the sweat from himself.

'Why now?' He turned onto his stomach and looked down at her. She was covered by the blanket now and her face was demure.

'Because in time to come, if I should ever think of you, I would like to have a name to fit to your face,' she said.

'Maudelyn Falcon.'

'Falcon?' her brow creased slightly, and she lay still for a moment. When she next spoke her voice was casual. 'You have not been at Court before?'

'Not these many years. I live in Kent at a place called Marie Regina.'

'With your wife.'

'With Diana, yes.' He had forgotten Diana, but what had just happened had nothing to do with Diana or his affection for her.

'Is she beautiful?' Louise asked. 'I hope she is beautiful?'

'Why?'

'Because it would be no compliment if you turned to me from a plain woman,' she said quaintly.

'She's beautiful,' he said. 'Older than you are, with a rosier skin and yellow hair.'

'Are you kind to her? I hope you're kind to her!'

'This is the first time I've been unfaithful to her since I married her, if that's what you mean,' he said dryly. 'But what of you?'

'I visit the Court from time to time,' she said in her vague manner, 'My husband is near sixty and has no youth left in him. No youth and no loving. The queen is kind and invites me to her private entertainments from time to time.'

'So that you may provide yourself with a stallion?' he asked coldly.

'Women have needs that must be satisfied too,' Louise said.

'And no morals,' he began, but she pulled his head down to hers, her sharp teeth biting into his ear, her supple body twisting and writhing beneath him and his own desire began to mount, and she was all the women he had ever known pressed down and running over.

The candle guttered lower, flared briefly, and went out. He slept, lean cheek on hand, sweat soaked hair dyed dark across the pillow. When he woke it was full day and the space beside him was empty.

For a moment he felt unreasonable anger, for she had used him and gone, leaving nothing of herself. Then he thought that it was no more than he had once done, tiptoeing out of a dozen bedrooms while his night's partner slept. And Louise had been honest with him, not asking for more than pleasure. It was strange that he should wake unsatisfied, for at Marie Regina, after he and Diana had made love, he rose feeling more loving.

He dressed, slapping briskness into his face from the bowl of water on the window ledge. This coming to Court had been an error of judgement. His true contentment lay at home with his wife. It had taken this journey to prove what Diana must have known all along. If he were wise, he'd ride back into Kent this very day.

'Maudelyn.' He knew the voice well and swung about, sinking to one knee as he recalled that his half brother was also his sovereign.

The king was wrapped in a fur mantle and there was more grey than red in his hair, but his square face was as Maudelyn remembered it.

'Get up, get up!' Henry's voice was irritable. 'No sense in standing on ceremony when we're alone! Joanna tells me that you've been here some little time.'

'About a week, sire.'

'I have not been well,' Henry said. 'An attack of ague that sometimes comes upon me in the spring. My soothsayer tells me that I will die in Jerusalem however. What do you make of that?'

'That Your Grace should take care never to go on Crusade,' Maudelyn said.

'And stay in England I will! My son now — he seeks leave to go to Burgundy. Scarcely a month since his return from Wales and he wants to be off again. Well, let him annoy the Burgundians and leave the citizens of London in peace. I am tired of his carousing.'

He spoke sourly with the pent up frustration of a sick man. There was no trace in his features of the characteristic blurring of the flesh that denoted leprosy but his hands were gloved, despite the warmth of the day. Maudelyn felt a shrinking in his own flesh.

'The prince has invited me to go to Burgundy with him,' he said.

'And I hope you will accept.' Henry's face had brightened slightly. 'There are days when I can trust nobody, nights when I dream of being toppled from my throne. Go to Burgundy, Maudelyn, and send back word to me of any treachery afoot.'

He dragged his furs more closely round himself and went out without a further word. A man eaten up by his own suspicions, Maudelyn thought, and pitied him. For old time's sake he would go with the prince but when the summer was drawing to a close he would return to Diana. And he would not seek out Louise again.

17

The thickset man with the rumpled grey hair paused as he approached the high tor and glanced up at the monastery. He remembered only too clearly how often he had toiled up the hill towards his lessons. Hated lessons when he had sat, longing to ride out into the green countryside, but bound to the declension of Latin verbs and the learning of the Ten Commandments. Well, he had broken most of them in the years since he had left Kent. The violence in his nature had been stirred and, to some extent, satisfied by the years of campaigning with his father, but violence was a habit with him now. He no longer tried to solve anything by reason, but he strode through the world taking what he wanted without thought or conscience — save for one thing.

He wanted Diana Maundy with a passion of which he had not believed himself capable. She had been, he sensed, the one woman with whom he might have settled, perhaps even be a better man. And Diana had listened to Roger Aston and run away from him.

It had given him pleasure to kill Roger. Pleasure to assure him that he would give up any idea of wedding the Maundy girl and pleasure to stab him deeply in the back as he turned to leave. But the Maundys were a different matter. He regretted having lost his temper with them, but could not feel that he was entirely to blame for their deaths. They had stood there so obstinately, declaring that they had no idea where Diana could be nor when she would return.

Despite having been cleared at the inquest of any suspicion of murder, and it had been his good fortune that the maidservant had been so terrifid by the sight of him in the courtroom that she had lost what wits she still possessed, he had never stopped looking over his shoulder ever since. Diana must have found out something of the Aston murder and fled. It was more than likely that she had thrown herself into the river long since. So he had been telling himself for years, and gradually both the hope and the fear of finding her had died. Until now.

Reining in his horse as he stared up at the dark mass of the monastery Godwin de Faucon pictured recent events. He had returned from the Continent ten years before, avoiding the city and the Court and anywhere that might bring him into contact with his family. He had taken a wife, a young heiress who had wept all the way to Church but who had brought with her a handsome manor house and a pleasant little fortune. She had also given him two children and, when he thought of Pierre and Jocasta, he hoped that his marriage had not been an unmitigated disaster. There was no doubt that he had never made Louise happy. He was well aware that her visits to Court were periods when she slaked her lust in the queen's private apartments with first one gallant and then another, but he cared little provided she was discreet and brought no scandal upon his name.

But this last episode had been different from the beginning. She had returned from a brief visit to Court in a strange, sulky mood, refusing even to play with the children. He had not paid much attention, but it was clear she had met someone who meant more to her than her usual admirers.

Then two weeks ago, he had come upon her weeping bitterly as she had not wept since their wedding day.

Moved by some impulse of pity he had touched her shoulder and she flung away from his hand as if he carried a branding iron.

'What ails you?' he asked.

'A letter from a friend at Court — ' she began.

'A man?' he interrupted.

'A lady, but she sends news of a gentleman. He went to Burgundy last month with Prince Hal and died there — died in a few days from a fever brought on by the bite of a fly.'

'I take it the gentleman was also a friend of yours,' he said sombrely.

'I met him once,' she said, her reticence destroyed by her shocked grief. 'Just the one night.'

'Then you won't recall his name, among so many.'

'It was Falcon,' she said. 'Maudelyn Falcon. It sounded so much like de Faucon that I was startled for a moment.'

'What did he look like, this Maudelyn Falcon?'

'Younger than you,' she said cruelly. 'Tall and fair with eyes like green grass. Able to give a woman pleasure.'

'Has he no wife to occupy his nights?' he asked.

'At his home in Kent. A place called Marie Regina — yes, that was it. He talked about her a little. Her name is Diana and this was the first time he'd been unfaithful to her in all their married life. You're hurting me!'

She ended in a gasp of pain as he caught

hold of her wrist, twisting it viciously.

'His wife's name? What was his wife's name?'

'Diana. I told you!'

'Her second name. Did he give her second name?'

'Maundy. He said it was Maundy. What does it matter?' She was sobbing now with terror as well as grief.

'So!' He released her abruptly and strode out of the room.

At that moment he could not have told whether anger or fear were uppermost in his mind. Diana was still alive and married to his own nephew, to Gida's bastard! It was startling but it fitted into the pattern, just as it fitted into the pattern that Maudelyn should have seduced Louise.

He had said nothing more to Louise; had even spoken to her kindly; had made it clear that he would never mention the episode to her again. Maudelyn was dead, and he was thus denied the satisfaction of killing him. But Diana still lived. Diana had spurned him and married his bastard nephew. Diana must be aware of the truth about her parents' deaths. Yet she had hidden herself in the one place where he had never thought of going. There was a grim humour in that, but he had no leisure as yet in which to savour it.

He had ridden into Kent by easy stages, giving false names at the inns where he stayed along the way. He rode alone, without escort, his hat pulled low over his eyes, a plain cloak shielding him from the breeze. As he rode so the rage within him grew colder and harder until there was room for no other emotion.

A figure was coming down the winding path towards the bridge. He peered through the darkness, one hand clutching the hilt of his dagger. The moon was rising and for a moment the landscape was lit up as if it were full day, and in that moment he saw her clearly. She was no longer the young girl he had desired but a ripe and lovely woman with fulfilment in every curve. Her hair was loose and glinted silver and her face was the face he remembered.

Maudelyn had married this woman had held her in his arms enjoying her soft flesh and yielding mouth. Maudelyn had taken Louise too, leaving her after one night, and Louise had wept for him. She had wept when Godwin married her, wept when Maudelyn died.

He rode forward into the clearing, the moonlight gleaming on his dagger. He was not aware of having drawn it, not aware of anything save the urgent need to possess.

Diana both heard and saw the man that

followed her and for an instant his face was etched in the moonlight like some terrible and primitive carving. Then she was running across the bridge, her breath sobbing in her throat, her hair streaming behind her, the sound of her own heart beating in her ears.

It was like that other time when she had been little, clutching the seal, holding Becky's hand. She stumbled and fell to her knees and the high scream of the rearing horse drowned her own shriek.

Hoof struck against bone and the horse stood trembling, sweat lathered. Godwin dismounted and stared down at the wide open eyes, the dull bruise on the temple. Someone was running down the hill behind him. He turned, without surprise, to face Gida's small, cloaked figure.

'I did not mean to hurt her,' he said stiffly. 'I meant to put away my wife and marry her.'

'Diana was already wed,' Gida told him.

'To your bastard. I know. He died in Burgundy some weeks past. I'm surprised the news has not reached you yet.'

'Maudelyn dead?' Her voice was a thread of sound.

'Aye, dead.' He spoke brutally, glad to feel his power over her. She had always looked down on him even when they were children because she had been clever at her lessons.

'He has only been away for a little while,' she said blankly. 'I can't believe — did you?'

'He died of a fever. I had nothing to do with it.'

'And this?' She looked down at the sprawled body.

'Not my fault,' he said harshly. 'I meant her no harm. As God is my witness — '

'Don't call upon God,' she interrupted. 'He has no part in this.'

'I meant to wed her long ago but she fled me.' He was justifying himself as he had often done in the past when he neglected his lessons or gone coney snaring. 'She ran away from me. I didn't mean to kill her. It was an accident. She fell and my horse reared. You must have seen it.'

'Marry her? You to marry Diana?' Suddenly, shockingly, Gida began to laugh, flinging back her head, her eyes closed.

'Stop it!' He shook her roughly. 'Stop laughing!'

'But you don't understand,' she gasped. 'You don't understand how funny it is. Look at her, fool! *Look at her!* Doesn't she remind you of somebody? Her hair is your colour, my dear brother. Her face — look at her face, Godwin! Petrella was dark but her hair curled at her temples in exactly that way.'

'Petrella died,' he said hoarsely. 'She died in child-birth.'

'But the child lived. I named her Diana. She lived.'

'Then how came she to be Maundy?' he cried. 'You seek to confuse me with your lies!'

'No lie,' Gida said, and she was no longer laughing. 'You abandoned Petrella and broke Ralph Aston's heart, and I brought her here to Marie Regina. She died here and Diana was born here. Then the peasants came. She was a tiny girl but they took her with them and killed Becky, her nursemaid. For years she was lost to me, until Maudelyn brought her home as his bride. He never knew who she really was — he never knew she was your daughter.'

'I have two other children,' he mumbled. 'Pierre and Jocasta. Good children.'

'You had a third,' she said ruthlessly. 'You have killed her.'

'By accident. I swear — '

'Have done with swearing,' she interrupted. 'Help me put her over the horse. I'll tell them she was thrown.'

He obeyed her silently, his big hands shaking. Diana's body was chilled by the wind. When he tried to close her eyes the

323

lids resisted his fingers and her blank stare burned into his brain.

'I will ride home,' Gida said. She spoke calmly as if she were already past grief, and all business between them was at an end.

'Gida.' He had not known his voice could plead.

'Godwin?' Mounted on her pony she looked at him from within the shadow of her hood.

'We are both old now, near the end of our lives. I have a wife and children.'

'And this was an accident. So you said.'

She gave him a long last look and was gone, riding into the shadow beyond the bridge, leading the other mount with its limp burden. Godwin remounted and glanced back at the tor, wondering why the two women should have been visiting the monastery so late. For some inexplicable reason fear swept over him and he gritted his teeth to stop the trembling of his jaw. Then he jerked at the rein and galloped back the way he had come as if the devil were at his heels.

A month later Gida stood with the four children by the newly dug grave. The ground had not yet settled and only a simple wooden cross marked the place. Winter was drawing in before its time and Alice and Alfreda were muffled in fur trimmed velvet mantles. They stood, hand in hand, looking down at the bunch of hawthorn they had just laid on the soil.

'I want you to remember what I say to you,' Gida said softly. 'I want you to remember it all your lives. Your lady mother lies here before her due time, cut off like the hawthorn. She will not rest until she is avenged. That is the task the dead lay upon the living. It is a task you must fulfil.'

'How, grandmother?' William asked.

'There is a man,' Gida said. 'His name is Godwin de Faucon. Never forget that name. Godwin de Faucon. He has a wife, called — I don't know how she is called, but 'tis no matter. And he has children, two children. They are our enemies. All of them are enemies. When you are older you will take your revenge upon them.'

'Yes, grandmother.' John stood up very straight, his clear young eyes fixed on the small, grey-haired figure.

'Swear it upon the soul of your mother,' Gida said. 'Clasp hands and swear.'

Four hands reached to clasp and entwine, Alfreda giggling as her plump little fingers were clutched in Alice's palm.

'Good-morrow, Mistress Falcon.' The Abbot was coming towards them, his long robe fluttering about him.

'My Lord Abbot.' Gida curtsied, her eyes lowered respectfully.

'A melancholy visit,' he observed. 'Have the children been into chapel yet?'

'Indeed, my lord, but they have prayed most fervently,' she assured him.

'Then run along to the refectory. Brother Anselm has hot ginger wine and cinnamon cakes for you.'

He smiled indulgently as they scampered away, the boys ahead of their sisters.

'Children are very resilient,' Gida said.

'Not only children.' He permitted himself a glance of admiration. 'You have been dealt a crushing blow. Yet you rise above it. That is true nobility of character.'

'The children are my responsibility,' she said. 'It's my duty to rear them as Maudelyn and Diana would have wished.'

'We will extend your lease on the castle for as long as it is required,' he said.

'You are most generous.'

'And the children will receive their schooling here, of course.'

'You are very kind,' she said. 'I would like all of them to have a good education. I never regretted mine.'

'I'll warrant you were an excellent student,' he said.

'And life has taught me many lessons

since.' She looked down again at the hawthorn blossom and her lips curved into a smile.

'You still have much to live for,' the Abbot said.

'Oh, indeed,' she agreed softly. 'Why, my lord, I begin to feel as if my task were only just beginning!'

THE END

McLEAN AT THE GOLDEN OWL
George Goodchild

Inspector McLean has resigned from Scotland Yard's CID and has opened an office in Wimpole Street. With the help of his able assistant, Tiny, he solves many crimes, including those of kidnapping, murder and poisoning.

KATE WEATHERBY
Anne Goring

Derbyshire, 1849: The Hunter family are the arrogant, powerful masters of Clough Grange. Their feuds are sparked by a generation of guilt, despair and ill-fortune. But their passions are awakened by the arrival of nineteen-year-old Kate Weatherby.

A VENETIAN RECKONING
Donna Leon

When the body of a prominent international lawyer is found in the carriage of an intercity train, Commissario Guido Brunetti begins to dig deeper into the secret lives of the once great and good.

A TASTE FOR DEATH
Peter O'Donnell

Modesty Blaise and Willie Garvin take on impossible odds in the shape of Simon Delicata, the man with a taste for death, and Swordmaster, Wenczel, in a terrifying duel. Finally, in the Sahara desert, the intrepid pair must summon every killing skill to survive.

SEVEN DAYS FROM MIDNIGHT
Rona Randall

In the Comet Theatre, London, seven people have good reason for wanting beautiful Maxine Culver out of the way. Each one has reason to fear her blackmail. But whose shadow is it that lurks in the wings, waiting to silence her once and for all?

QUEEN OF THE ELEPHANTS
Mark Shand

Mark Shand knows about the ways of elephants, but he is no match for the tiny Parbati Barua, the daughter of India's greatest expert on the Asian elephant, the late Prince of Gauripur, who taught her everything. Shand sought out Parbati to take part in a film about the plight of the wild herds today in north-east India.